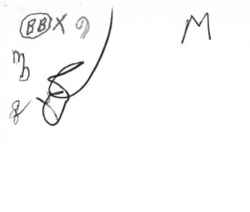

COWBOY FOR A
RAINY AFTERNOON

**Center Point
Large Print**

Also by Stephen Bly and available from Center Point Large Print:

The Land Tamers
Creede of Old Montana

This Large Print Book carries the Seal of Approval of N.A.V.H.

COWBOY FOR A RAINY AFTERNOON

RAINY

AFTERNOON

Stephen Bly

CENTER POINT PUBLISHING
THORNDIKE, MAINE

This Center Point Large Print edition
is published in the year 2010
by arrangement with the author.

First edition, June 2010

The text of this Large Print edition is unabridged.
Printed in the United States of America.
Set in 16-point Times New Roman type.

ISBN: 978-1-60285-673-8

Library of Congress Cataloging-in-Publication Data

Bly, Stephen A., 1944–
   Cowboy for a rainy afternoon / Stephen Bly. — 1st ed.
      p. cm.
   ISBN 978-1-60285-673-8 (library binding : alk. paper)
   1. Grandfathers—Fiction. 2. Grandsons—Fiction. 3. Albuquerque (N.M.)—Fiction.
   4. New Mexico—History—20th century—Fiction. 5. Large type books. I. Title.
   PS3552.L93C67 2010
   813′.54—dc22
2010000061

COWBOY FOR A
RAINY AFTERNOON

CHAPTER 1

The Matador Hotel died on July 5, 1965, but they didn't bother burying it until last fall.

New Mexico heat blanketed Albuquerque that July like too many covers in a stuffy cabin. The kind of day that you sweat from the inside out and feel sticky dirt in places that you don't ponder much except in the shower. I reckon that four-bladed overhead fan that squeaked like an unfed cat failed to console Shorty McGuire. Doc Boyce said he passed on durin' the night, but no one discerned it until they observed the empty back table at the Round-Up Café. For the last nineteen years of his life, Shorty lived in a second-floor room at the Matador. At straight up 6:00 a.m. ever' mornin', he ate two eggs fried hard under the faded picture of Theodore Roosevelt leading the Rough Riders up San Juan Hill.

As a boy, I calculated that Shorty McGuire and the others must be pushing a hundred-years-old when I met them for the first time in 1954.

I reckon I surmised wrong.

The *Albuquerque Herald* reported that Hadley (Shorty) McGuire was only eighty-six when he died on that July day in 1965. The *Herald* is right most of the time.

As the last of that bunch at the Matador, there

was no one left to take his trappings, so Whip Johnson and me cleaned out Shorty's goods a few days after his funeral. Whip managed the hotel in the 60s for his Uncle Durwood Johnson who gained some fame in the Southwest on the rodeo circuit after the war. He won the hotel on a bet on a black, half-thoroughbred stallion down in Magdalena.

The floor of Shorty's little room with one four-pane slide-up window was carpeted solid with six to eight inches of newspapers, not a one newer than 1939. He claimed that cowboyin' didn't provide the time to read much, so he saved them for his retirement. I never did know if he got caught up.

We didn't have the nerve to give his tattered clothing to the Rescue Mission, so we chucked them into the hotel incinerator. We crated his boots, wooly chaps and battered Stetson, then donated them to the state museum. I had a notion they would want to display the gear of an old-time cowboy. But they stored them in a back room for a few years, then sold them at an auction to raise money for a modern art statue that looks like the scrap-iron pile out behind my barn. If I'd known they were selling Shorty's belongings, I'd have bought those suckers myself and buried them, rather than let some car dealer in Denver drive off with 'em. But that's the way the past is. You can't hang on to it all. What survives gets stolen by strangers who have no blasted idea of what they hold in their hands.

The tobacco-stained furniture in Shorty's room belonged to the hotel, but Whip decided to replace it all and re-carpet. So they moved in newer furniture, but I don't think the room was ever repainted. Whip and me always thought that room smelled like Lordsburg, but that might be its location on the south side of the hotel, facing the Santa Fe tracks.

I never went back to the hotel after that day. The hippies ran it in the early 70s, then some drug dealers. I think one of them big moving companies bought the place and used it for storage for a decade or two before they tore it down last year. All them red bricks got shipped to the west side for deluxe estate fencing around an upscale gated community. I hear they decided to build urban condos on the old hotel site for rich city folks, but I can't figure what kind of people would want to live in downtown Albuquerque.

At least, not nowadays.

I still have Shorty's rim-fire saddle hangin' in my tack room. It was one of the first ones Estaban Chavez built, when he still had that shop behind the Chinese laundry in Las Cruces. Lots of folks have wanted to buy it over the years, but it doesn't belong to me. Some day Shorty's kin will show up wantin' his things, and I'll have it ready.

9

I keep the leather oiled. Shorty died over forty years ago, but I'll hang onto it for him.

That's the way things are done around this part of the country.

It's one of the lessons I learned in the lobby of the Matador Hotel.

CHAPTER 2

I figure Shorty McGuire was seventy-five when I first met him on that rainy afternoon in 1954. He was the second youngest of the six men who lounged on those faded leather chairs and sofas. At seventy, my granddaddy ranked the youngest of the crew, yet they all called him Pop. The only one married at the time, Granddaddy was the only one not living at the Matador.

At ninety, Coosie Harte was the oldest and only lived a few months longer. To tell you the truth, age didn't mean a whole lot to a ten-year-old, but I do remember he pocketed his false teeth in his vest and packed a revolver in a worn holster on his hip. Later in life, it dawned on me that at Coosie's birth, Abraham Lincoln inhabited the White House. At twelve-years-old, Coosie read in the *Pecos Weekly Record* that Custer had been killed up on the Little Big Horn. And at thirty-five, he welcomed in the Twentieth Century.

That rainy afternoon, Granddaddy inherited the job of baby-sitting "Little Brother," as he called me. Every summer I spent two weeks with him and Grandma in a little one-bedroom house on 26th Street with a screened front porch and a mint plant growing on the north side next to the water hydrant. He took me to the Matador Hotel

11

that day where he liked to play cribbage with his cowboy pals. Grandma didn't cotton much to me going to the hotel for that reason. She viewed gambling cards as sinful. But Granddaddy propped me up on an orange crate and taught me cribbage when I was four. That day he let me wear my white straw cowboy hat, cap pistols and leather bullet belt with silver-painted wood bullets.

Cribbage and cowboys . . . I figured I fit right in.

Thad Brewer, the biggest of the bunch at three hundred pounds, seemed like a giant. He talked about fast horses and I could never imagine one big enough to tote him. I reckon he wasn't all that heavy when he was young. Thad lost a thumb on his right hand. When I asked Grandpa what happened to it, he just shook his head and said, "Little Brother, that's what happens to California dally men."

Quirt Payton wore a suit and tie with his narrow-brimmed Stetson and scuffed, underslung boots. The suit looked a hundred-years-old, but the tie always laid straight. Quirt had marshaled in several northern New Mexico towns. He made it a habit to sit with his back to the wall, eyes facin' the front door. He feared that some hombre he'd sent to jail would one day be paroled and come look for him. Quirt got run over and killed by one of those big Dodge cars with tailfins a few years later.

Most folks considered it an accident.

The sixth man of the crew went by the name Bronc. Even as a gray-haired, old man, his biceps bulged. His leather-tough, scarred face made a boy glad he was on my side. I never did know his last name. When I asked Granddaddy about it, he just said, "Little Brother, if Bronc wants you to know his last name, he'll tell you."

CHAPTER 3

The early May rain came down hard, the kind of cloudburst when the drops slap your face and you take it personal. I yanked my hat down and latched my stampede string tight under my chin. But I still got soaked by the time we pushed our way through a twelve-foot-tall door into a room that smelled of fine yellow dust and cheap cigar smoke.

Shorty McGuire saluted me first. "Pop, who's the fine lookin' cowboy you got with you today? Come here, son, and let me check out those pistols you're carryin'. I ought to get me some of these." He pondered them like they was first-generation, Colt single-action, army revolvers. "Yep, if I had me a couple of these, I wouldn't seem so out of place with Quirt and Coosie."

The elbows of Quirt Payton's wool suit coat were worn. He smelled of spice aftershave and dry-cleaning fluid. He kept one eye towards the front door after a quick glance at my cap pistols. "I was deputyin' in Globe City one time, when an old boy broke out of jail with a fake pistol he carved out of lye soap. Me and the sheriff was down at Patagonia on one of them fool Indian Tom chases. Melon Miles was the jailer in Globe.

He didn't know the gun was made out of soap, so he dove behind the oak desk so fast he busted two fingers on his right hand. Doc Ralston wanted to straighten out Miles's fingers with a rubber mallet, but ol' Melon declined. He should have listened to the doc. I saw him years later and them two fingers was as crooked as a faro dealer in Creede."

"Creede always treated me square," Coosie replied.

Thad Brewer rested his hands on his ample stomach. "Was that Johnny Appleseed who carved the gun and broke out of that Globe jail?"

"Yep, that's the one." Quirt pulled his crisp Stetson off and ran gnarled fingers through his thin, gray hair.

I felt my mouth gape open. I couldn't have been more stunned if they'd claimed Santa Claus got caught stealing candy at the five-and-dime. "Johnny Appleseed was in jail?" I gasped.

Shorty McGuire shoved my straw hat back. For a little man, he had the deepest laugh, one that makes you feel that everything is right with the world. His fingers felt as callused as alligator hide when he pinched my cheek. "Not THAT Johnny Appleseed, Little Brother. This ol' boy had some sort of affliction that made his face permanently red. Since his name was Johnny, folks started callin' him Johnny Apple or Appleseed. He rustled cattle, stole horses and cold-cocked drunks in the alley over in Arizony for a few years."

Bronc pulled out his red bandanna and blew a nose that reminded me of an oversized strawberry. As I look back, I don't reckon the sun caused it to be that color, but when you are ten, many a vice is overlooked.

It's one of the delightful insulations of childhood.

"Appleseed wasn't very good stealin', so he spent some time in jail," Bronc explained.

Quirt hooted, "I'll tell you one thing he was good at . . . carvin' pistols out of lye soap."

Like all the others, my granddaddy's white shirt was buttoned at the top, but he rolled up his sleeves as he talked. "He should have taken up carving. He could have done quite well." Granddaddy should know. He was the best carpenter and woodcarver of the bunch. He won a blue ribbon every year for his carving, until arthritis set in. I've still got a few of his Bernalillo County Fair ribbons in an old trunk out in the shop.

At least, I think they are still there.

CHAPTER 4

"Say, do you remember the time Johnny Appleseed stole a buckskin stallion from Sunny Bill over in Clifton, Arizona?" Coosie said. He pulled out a blue bandanna and coughed so deep I squinted my eyes closed. As a kid, I had no clue about advanced emphysema, but it sounded as if his lungs turned inside out.

Thad Brewer leaned forward and tapped a fat finger that seem to swallow his fingernail on the round table next to the cribbage board. "Sunny Bill was in Morenci."

"No, he was in Clifton." Coosie pulled out his teeth, rubbed his gums, and shoved the dentures inside his vest pocket.

"I wintered out '21 in Morenci. Sunny Bill operated that blacksmith shop right next to the High-Graders Saloon." Thad rubbed the place where his right thumb used to be. "The smithin' business turned meager, what with automobiles takin' over. Sunny Bill spent most of his days sittin' at the blue table near the back door at the High-Graders playin' poker. I remember the night he drew three queens to go with a pair of red trays and beat ol' Tombstone Tommy's three aces."

"I'm talkin' earlier than that." I had a hard time

17

not staring at Coosie's toothless mouth when he spoke. "Sunny Bill was in Clifton before the war." Coosie didn't have a hair on his round head. When he turned to me and winked, it was like looking at the man in the moon. "That was World War I, Little Brother." He chewed on his unlit cigar. "We called it the Great War back then."

Shorty's gray mustache sagged into a frown, but his eyes smiled. "Sunny Bill ran a livery business just west of the creek in Clifton. He bought and sold horses and mules. Mainly mules as I recall. They were still usin' a lot of 'em in the mines."

Quirt retrieved a wooden cribbage peg and cleaned his teeth. "I bought an ugly mule from Sunny Bill one time for five dollars. When I brought it back to the ranch, I thought the boys was goin' to die laughin'. Old Two-Fingered Oscar actually rolled in the dirt."

"I was with Oscar when he lost his fingers," Bronc reported.

"You were?" Granddaddy leaned back against the aging, brown, leather sofa. "You were down in Bisbee?" He pulled cigarette paper out of his shirt pocket, then looked down at me and smiled. I grinned 'cause that meant he'd stop by the store and buy me a nickel candy bar on the way home so I didn't tell Grandma he'd been smoking. It was a game we played. Grandma knew he smoked from the yellow stains on his fingers, but she figured it wasn't so bad if they never talked about it.

"It didn't happen in Bisbee," Bronc corrected. "It was up in the mountains east of Tombstone."

"You're right, Bronc. Runny Peters was the one who lost his fingers in Bisbee," Granddaddy said.

Thad took a sip of coffee from a thick, porcelain mug and grimaced. At least, as a lad, I assumed it was coffee. "Runny had that ol' Spencer blow up on him, didn't he?"

Quirt yanked off his gold, wire-framed glasses and rubbed the bridge of his nose. "Those black powder guns aren't built for smokeless powder. Lot of them blew up, especially in a gunfight when the barrel got too hot."

A cold chill slid down my back beneath the rain-dampened, gingham shirt. I pulled out one of my pressed-metal cap pistols and studied it.

"Don't worry, Little Brother," Coosie rasped. "You got yourself a fine gun. It won't explode. You can tell a lot about a man by the quality of firearm he packs."

CHAPTER 5

The massive front door of the Matador squeaked open as a uniformed delivery boy carried a huge, dark-blue vase of multi-colored, spring flowers over to the registration desk.

Nearly five-hundred combined years of crease-eyed cowboy experience followed the man across the lobby.

"Did somebody die?" Coosie asked, as he half-stuffed his bandanna back into his pocket.

"I bet they're for that young girl ol' Johnson hired to keep the hotel books," Shorty pondered.

Coosie snorted. "This is the only place in town where a thirty-five-year-old woman can come to work and be considered a young girl." He reached into his coat pocket, pulled several pepper-mints, then rolled them across the table toward me as if they were dice. I glanced at Granddaddy. He nodded, so I shoved one in my mouth.

Quirt pushed his narrow-brimmed Stetson back, then slipped on his glasses. "Her name is Diane Anderson and she's only thirty-one."

The men turned to stare at the retired marshal.

"I got to know who's surrounding me, boys," he explained, "if I aim to live as long as Coosie."

The men grinned as if they knew a secret that they weren't about to discuss.

"Tell us about ol' Oscar," Granddaddy ventured into the long pause.

Bronc cleared his throat like a man used to dangling a cigarette from his lips. "Oscar and me worked the fall gather for Charley Seque on the Quarter-Circle R down in the Dragoon Mountains. Me, Oscar and Charley rode up Willow Wash chasin' rustlers. We got them cornered right above the tanks. Oscar pinned them down with that Winchester 1894 38/55 carbine of his while . . ."

"That was a fine gun," Shorty interrupted. "Had a half magazine and a shotgun butt, if I recollect."

"That's the one," Bronc replied.

Quirt Payton rested his hand on the polished walnut handle of his holstered revolver until the delivery boy pushed his way back out into the scattered rain of the New Mexico noon. "Did you know that gun is under the bar at the Lead Bucket Saloon in Bisbee?" he said.

"What's it doing there?" Granddaddy asked.

"J.T. claims he's saving it in case Oscar's family ever comes looking for his goods," Quirt explained.

"Like I said," Bronc continued, "Oscar had them rustlers pinned down in the rocks while me and Charley circled the stolen bovines and drove them down the hill to Cholla Springs."

"Cholla Springs?" Coosie jammed another

21

peppermint into his toothless mouth. "That's where Loop Randerhoff crossed the great divide, ain't it?"

"No, that was in Cholla Springs, New Mexico," Bronc explained. "I'm talkin' Arizona."

Coosie rubbed his bald head as if there was hair to brush back. "He was one hard workin' pard. Did any of you ever work an outfit with Loop?"

CHAPTER 6

"Me and Loop pushed eight-hundred head up to the Navajo at Window Rock in ought nine," Thad offered.

Coosie raised his thick eyebrows. It gave him a jack-o'-lantern look. "You was in that crew?"

"Yep. Me and him rode point. He was a good hand. Loop never complained about anything," Thad Brewer murmured. "Unlike some I won't mention."

Shorty ignored the dig and spun the warped cribbage board on the table like a roulette wheel. "Was you there when the major broke his neck?"

Thad's voice softened. "Me and Loop dug the grave."

"You don't say?" Quirt said. "How come you never told us that?"

"It ain't a day I like to recollect," Thad admitted.

Granddaddy patted his bony hand on my shoulder. My gingham shirt still felt damp. "The major was the finest horseman I ever seen." He shook his head like a man who had just lost his wife.

"I'll agree to that," Coosie chimed in. "Whatever happened to that long-legged, black stallion of his?"

Granddaddy plucked up the last peppermint and handed it to me. "I heard a banker from El Paso bought him and hauled him in a train car all the way home. When he got there, his boy led the stallion out of the car. The horse bolted and dashed right for the river, dragging the boy with him. The banker ran after them hollering 'hold on to him, son, don't let go.' The stallion dragged that poor kid for about a half-mile and then hit the river. The boy let go."

Bronc laughed. "Don't reckon the ol' man was tickled."

Granddaddy's smile revealed cigarette stains on his lips and teeth. "They say the horse swam over to Mexico and sprinted towards the Diablo Mountains still draggin' the lead rope. I heard that the daddy wouldn't speak to the son for a year. They never recovered the horse."

Shorty stretched out his legs. I could see his socks peek through a hole in his worn brown boots. "It's sort of nice to think about the major's stallion finishin' his life runnin' wild down in the Diablos, maybe with a band of wild mares trottin' behind him."

Coosie's voice was a raspy whisper. "It surely beats endin' up bein' an ol' man alone in a small room at the Matador Hotel, don't it?"

The lobby got so quiet I could hear the rain pelting the tin awnings over the windows out front. The ceiling fan lapped at the flies high over our heads. The aroma of smoke and dust reminded me of an old barn that no longer housed animals bigger than a cat.

Quirt Payton's leather-tough hands wiped the corners of his eyes. "Dadgum dust is so thick in here it's a wonder some Oklahoma sharecroppers ain't moved in and rock-cornered a claim."

My eyes darted from one old man to the next ponderin' who was going to speak next. I understand now the sadness in their eyes that afternoon. There comes a point in ever' man's life when the reckless freedom of youth sours into the gnawing loneliness of old age.

CHAPTER 7

Bronc pulled himself to his feet and shuffled over to the office behind the counter of the hotel lobby. With his massive shoulders, he didn't stroll through the doorway. He turned sideways and slipped through like a big pill and too little water.

Shorty McGuire cleared his throat. "The major broke his neck when he got bucked off, ain't that right?"

Thad Brewer stiffened his sagging shoulders. "No sir, don't you believe that for a minute. I know some say that, but the major could ride a cougar with a hatpin in its rear end. No sir, he stuck like pine tar to a saddle. He took a fall that day when his ol' McGee broke."

"How's that?" Granddaddy prodded.

"Like I said, we had six men and were movin' eight-hundred head up to the reservation. You know how the major was a stickler for gettin' ever' cow delivered. He wouldn't lose a one. We had a skinny sack-of-bones cow that wandered down a steep barranca and couldn't get out. Loop Randerhoff and me tried ridin' down after it, but the drop-off was too steep and brushy. That scrawny steer hid in the brush and bawled like a Hereford yearling separated from its mama for the first time. We should have just shot it and fed the coyotes."

"How did the cow get down there?" I asked.

Coosie looked at me so intently that I began to chew on my tongue. His voice stayed soft, yet unrelenting, like an afternoon summer breeze up in the San Juan Mountains. "Them cows is mysterious animals, Little Brother. They can disappear before your very eyes, then materialize in the wildest places. They ain't human, you know."

Granddaddy rubbed my shoulder with strong, bony fingers. Bronc returned with his white shirt partially tucked in and carried a steaming glass pitcher of coffee.

"Man at the pot," Coosie mumbled as Bronc made the rounds of pouring coffee.

He set the rest of the coffee in front of me. "You can drink straight out of the pitcher, if you want to, Little Brother." He grinned, then collapsed back on the old leather divan.

"Did you get that cow out of the barranca?" I prodded.

Thad fanned out a deck of cards, then flipped them over like collapsing dominos. None of the old, worn, blue deck had any numbers. "The major told us not to. He dismounted, tied a rope around a mesquite tree on the rim, and let himself down into the brushy barranca. Come to find out, three cows were hidin' in that gully. Two were plumb wild, unbranded, and stampeded the major. He pulled out his pistol and fired over their heads. All three turned tail and struck a nine for the other end of the barranca. Before you can say Poncho Villa, they plowed through the thorn bush and up the southern slope. We bunched 'em up and turned them back with the herd."

"So you gained two cows?" I said.

Thad's voice grew quiet again. "What we lost was worth more than a dozen herds, boys."

CHAPTER 8

"What happened to the major?" I asked.

Thad flipped the cards over and shuffled them, never taking his hands off the table. "Rather than follow the cow trail all the way through that brush to risk bein' sliced to ribbons by the thorns, the major climbed hand-over-fist up that McGee tied to the mesquite trunk."

I tugged on my granddaddy's sleeve. "What's a McGee?"

"It's a rope, Little Brother," Granddaddy whispered. "Made from the century plant, but it ain't too strong when it's tied hard and fast."

Thad Brewer rubbed his hand on the place where God had created a right thumb. "The major almost made it to the top when that McGee busted. He tumbled back like a sack of oats and hit his head on a rock no bigger than a doorstop. There wasn't ten rocks down there, and he had to bust his head on one of them. It don't seem fair, does it?"

"Life ain't always fair." Shorty brushed his thick mustache, but didn't look up.

Thad shook his head and stared out the smeared glass window that faced the street. "It took us five, maybe ten minutes to hack our way through the thorn brush and get to him. The major was dead by the time we got there. I ain't ashamed to say it, boys, but I cried and cried that day."

Coosie Harte picked at his ear with his little finger as if he had ticks. "Some things is worth cryin' over."

"Must have took us two hours to haul him up. Me and Loop dug a deep grave under that forked cottonwood south of Adobe Springs," Thad said.

Shorty was still rubbing his mustache when he looked up. "The major is buried near Adobe Springs?"

Thad spread out the deck face down, then pulled out a card. "His folks came and dug him up the next April and took him back home to Tennessee." He flipped the card over on top of the table. It was the king of clubs. "Of course, me and the boys had us a service that day when we buried him. I reckon the Good Lord got himself a fine ranahan the day the major went to heaven. Oregon Sam was ridin' with us and he sang hymns over the major's grave."

Quirt Payton reached for the line of cards and plucked one up. "I have never heard finer hymns than how ol' Sam sang them." He flipped over the king of diamonds.

Coosie rubbed his full lips, then leaned over and grabbed a card. "Pop, did you ever hear Sam sing *Annie Laurie*?" He uncovered the king of hearts.

Granddaddy walked his fingers along the cards like a mouse full of yellow cheese. "I reckon that's the sweetest sound this side of heaven." He pointed to a card and nodded for me to turn it over.

My eyes widened as I exposed the king of spades.

"Anyway," Thad continued, "we buried the major and ended up in Window Rock with two extra cows. We made sure we didn't lose a one."

Coosie flopped back and sipped on his coffee. "Trouble is, we've buried most of 'em, boys."

"Yep," Shorty said, "we're the lucky ones."

Bronc wiped coffee drips off his chin with the back of his hand. "Yeah, we're the lucky ones, alright."

CHAPTER 9

The bent, brass bell tinkled when the oak and smudged-glass, front door of the Matador swung open. A weak-eyed man, wearing pointed-toe cowboy boots and a wide-brimmed, rain-streaked, white Stetson sauntered across the lobby to the registration counter. Quirt Payton reached for the grip of his old, single-action, army revolver. I had to lean forward to peer around the large, plaster pillar that blocked my view. All six men fixed their eyes on the man.

"Yeah, most of the ol' bunch is gone," Shorty continued, "but I reckon part of 'em is still alive, as long as we remember them."

"And tell cowpokes like Little Brother all about 'em." Coosie watched the man in the white cowboy hat lean across the counter and visit with the blonde bookkeeper, who had slipped out of the back room.

Quirt relaxed his stiff fingers off the gun and tapped on the table. He stared right through me, his voice like a schoolteacher givin' a test. "Little Brother, don't you ever forget men like the major . . . or Loop Randerhoff, for that matter."

Granddaddy grabbed my arm until it hurt. "Someday, Little Brother, it will be your turn to tell these stories to your kids and your grand-kids. Tell them true, 'cause the history books won't."

"Ain't that fer sure," Shorty blurted out. "History books are written by people who weren't there but think they know ever'thin'."

Thad Brewer nodded at the whispered conversation at the front desk, then raised his eyebrows as if to say "who is that guy?"

Bronc pointed to a card in the middle of the table. He motioned for me to turn it over. "Did they ever catch Loop's killer?" he asked.

I turned over a coffee-stained joker.

"I don't reckon so," Quirt said. "Least, I haven't heard."

Shorty leaned back in the divan and plunked his boots up on the table. They were as creased as his face. "Did they ever ascertain what happened to old Loop?"

"A man lives with his past. You cain't outrun it forever." Quirt Payton kept one eye on the man at the counter, reminding me of Gary Cooper's stare in *High Noon*. I imagined that if the man stormed towards us, we'd have a gunfight right there in the lobby of the Matador.

"Loop was purdy wild as a lad." Granddaddy's Adam's apple bobbed up and down in unison with the narrow brim of his old Stetson. "He got chased out of Telluride more than once. I know that for a fact."

"Shoot, who hasn't?" Bronc thundered.

They all laughed, but Quirt. He studied the man in the white hat.

Coosie leaned forward and turned over another joker. "One July, I hit it big at the faro table and went to the finest hotel in Telluride and ordered me a room. They wouldn't let me stay there. Said I wasn't their kind."

"I thought all it took was money," Bronc said.

Thad Brewer let out a deep laugh that plastered me against the back of my chair. "You don't suppose they wanted you to take a bath?"

"Dadgumit, that's why a man checks into a hotel . . . to take a bath and clean up," Coosie said. "It's not like they never smelled manure on boots before."

Shorty leaned his head back and closed his eyes. "I reckon you soured just a tad. Did you shoot up the place that time, Coosie?"

Coosie pointed a finger, like a gun, at the yellowed, dusty chandelier in the middle of the ceiling. "Nope. It was '05 and they didn't tolerate boys that hurrahed a place."

"That's one of the troubles with modern times," Bronc added. "There is no place left for a good hurrahin'. I always figured a lot of trouble was avoided when you let the cowboys hurrah."

The man at the counter laughed loud enough

that all the old men paused and glanced at him. As I think back, it was one of them explosive laughs, not a reaction to humor, but almost a statement of anger . . . or lust.

CHAPTER 10

Quirt loosened his black tie. I could see the yellowed collar of his white shirt still buttoned at the top. "Loop did more than a little hurrahin' in his day. He shot up a gambling house in Telluride and left a few men dead."

"A few? How many is a few?" I croaked.

"One to five is a few," Granddaddy told me. "Leaving seven to ten dead is a lot."

"And leavin' more than ten dead," Bronc roared, "is a dadgum lie!"

"So did one of them that Loop leaded down have kin that settled the score?" Thad questioned.

The conversation at the lobby counter increased in volume. We all stared at the book-keeper shaking her head and her fist.

Quirt Payton slipped his revolver out of the holster. I couldn't keep my eyes off the nine notches in the walnut grip. I pulled out my cap pistol and looked at the smooth, white, plastic grips.

"You expectin' trouble, Quirt?" Coosie wheezed, his hand on his own holstered revolver.

My heart pounded. Like Quirt Payton, I slowly cocked the hammer back on my cap gun with my right thumb.

"Nope. Just thinkin' about ol' Loop, I reckon. A

delivery boy for that old Green River Grocery found him face down in the mud. A shotgun blast to the back. I reckon it was all over in a hurry. At least, the delivery boy said he found him that way."

"Quirt, you don't have to worry about being shot in the back," Thad hooted. "Ain't no one seen your back since before Prohibition."

"Of course," Shorty added, "it only takes one mistake."

"That's right," Coosie said. "Just remember ol' Bill Hickok."

The conversation at the counter grew louder and more animated, but I couldn't make out any of the words. "Mr. Harte, did you know Wild Bill Hickok?" I asked.

He seemed to stare right past the wall and the decades. "I was just a pup back then. I never met the man. But I must have met five-hundred men who were at the Number 10 Saloon in Deadwood on the day he got shot in the back of the head."

"Five-hundred?" I said. "I didn't know saloons were that big."

"They ain't, Little Brother," Granddaddy said. "Everybody wants to pretend they were there when history happened. But most of us don't witness much but the routine."

"Miss Diane is sure wound up tight." Quirt nodded towards the counter. "She talks with her hands a lot when she's riled."

"I had me a gal named Margarita, once, who talked a lot with her hands," Shorty blurted out.

"Big Margarita down at Columbus?" Bronc asked.

"Yep." Shorty grinned. "She surely had large hands."

Thad whooped. "She had large ever'thin'!"

"I asked Big Margarita to marry me six times one night." Bronc laughed.

Shorty sat straight up and yanked off his hat. "You did?"

"Yep," Bronc hooted. "Her and every other woman in the cantina."

"And they all turned you down?" I asked.

Bronc grinned. "It was my lucky night."

Quirt balanced his revolver on the worn, slick knee of his suit pants. I couldn't tell if he had bullets in five or all six chambers. "I heard she cold-cocked one of Villa's men when they made that raid across the border."

"She cold-cocked his horse," Shorty reported.

I swallowed hard and jammed my cap gun back into the holster. "His horse?"

"Yep, that Mexican hit the ground runnin' towards the border. He might still be running," Shorty said. "Not even Poncho Villa could face the wrath of Big Margarita with a lead pipe in her hand."

"Is she the ol' gal who gave you that black eye?" Granddaddy asked.

Shorty sighed, then nodded. "Two of them."

"She gave you two black eyes?" I quizzed.

Shorty shrugged. "Little Brother, some men is slow learners."

CHAPTER 11

"Here he comes," Thad murmured.

Shorty sat up.

Quirt laid his hand on his revolver.

The thin man with the white cowboy hat ambled toward the front door.

Coosie coughed into his bandanna, then called out, "What outfit you ride for, son?"

The man stopped, turned, then sneered. "Did you ask me something?"

"Coosie wants to know what ranch you work on," Shorty said.

The man strolled over to the old men on the brown sofas. "Ranch work?"

Thad stretched out his fat fingers and cracked his knuckles. "We can tell by your fine hat and boots you must be a cowboy."

He offered a crooked tooth grin. "Oh, yeah, I'm a cowboy."

When Bronc's brown eyes sparkled, the creases melted. "Do you work out on the Pecos, boy? There are still some good spreads out there. Maybe up near Las Vegas, but they hire mainly Mexican vaqueros now."

The man's thin mustache looked more like a smudge. It reminded me of the one on that lady barber over at Clayton. "Oh, no," he explained. "I don't work on a ranch."

Quirt pulled out a tin of Copenhagen and eased off the lid as if it were full of gold dust. "Where do you work?"

The man beamed. "At the Standard Oil filling station on Indian School Road."

With some amount of effort, Thad Brewer leaned forward and turned the two jokers face down. "You own a filling station? That's quite an accomplishment for a young man. I'm proud of you, son."

When the man shoved his hat back, it pushed his ears out to a humorous position. There was no tan line on his forehead. "Own it? Oh, I don't own it. But I am manager of the flat-tire shop."

"That's a very fine accomplishment," Granddaddy replied with his patented, straight face. When I was young, I thought he could have been a world-champion, poker player with that uncommitted stare. Of course, Grandma would never have allowed that.

Shorty McGuire could barely contain his glee. He covered his thin-lipped smile. "We naturally assumed from that fine hat and nobby boots that you was ridin' the range."

The man pulled off his hat. His blond butch haircut stood like barley stubble after harvest. "Isn't this a dandy? It cost me twenty dollars. I ordered it and these boots all the way from Nudie's. Nothing but the best for Leon Herbert."

41

Quirt jammed a pinch of Copenhagen between his cheek and gum, then closed the lid on the little round box. "Nudie's?"

"Yep, I mail ordered them C.O.D. all the way from North Hollywood, California. That's the same store that Rex Allen buys his boots. Ol' Nudie makes boots and clothes for all them famous movie stars."

"You don't say?" Thad rolled his eyes towards me.

"Tip Hardy's boy ran government beef with Rex Allen's uncle one summer on the Rim near San Carlos," Bronc said. "He said Rex was makin' a hand before he ran off to those picture shows."

"Was his name Tad?" Coosie asked.

"No, Tip's boy was named Todd," Quirt corrected. "He used to rope left-handed. Won a lot of money up at the Prescott Rodeo one summer. Dismounted from the off side. I wonder why more boys don't do that?"

"Tip was a purdy good rodeo hand in his day, too," Shorty added.

"Remember that overo paint horse ol' Tip had? It surely attracted the ladies when he rode into town," Thad mused. "I remember one time me and . . ."

"I've got me a nearly new '53 Mercury," Leon blurted out. "It's quite the lady killer, if you remember what I mean."

"Tip and me rode into Benson on a Saturday night," Thad continued.

"It's two-tone . . . Dutch-cream white and wheat-harvest gold," Leon reported.

Thad shifted his large frame to the front of the sofa. "Tip had two invitations to supper and a half-dozen, pig-tailed girls wantin' to ride double before we tied up to the rail. And all because of that dadgum paint horse of his. It's no wonder he called that cow-pony Romeo."

"I almost got me one of them convertibles," Leon spurted. "But, there are times a girl enjoys a little more privacy . . . ain't that right?"

Coosie pulled his teeth out of his pocket and slipped them into this mouth. He sure looked different with teeth. "Thad, I surmise you ate supper alone that night."

"I didn't see Tip until Monday." Thad laughed.

"Of course, Tip was a handsome man," Shorty said. "Until he got hit by the California Flyer."

"He was run over by a train?" I asked.

"Not run over, Little Brother," Shorty said. "But he never did look or walk the same after that."

"Eh, did you old men want anything else?" Leon mumbled.

"I reckon you got to get back to them flat tires," Bronc said.

"I'm not goin' back today," Leon reported. "I got me a big date."

Shorty glanced back at the empty, hotel registration desk. "Treat her like a lady, son."

"What?"

"Miss Diane is a friend of ours," Quirt said. "We jist want you to treat her square."

Leon surveyed the lobby of the Matador Hotel. He lowered his voice. "Shoot, I ain't goin' with Diane. I'm goin' out with Teresa who dances down at the Day-Lyte Club."

Quirt fingered the revolver.

"Payton," Coosie cautioned. "Relax."

Leon Herbert started towards the front door, then spun back. "Say, were you old men real cowboys once?"

"I reckon we were," Granddaddy replied.

The man whistled as he tugged the brim of his hat down and strolled outside into the drizzle.

CHAPTER 12

Bronc pulled a spittoon to the front of the leather chair. From the sound, his was not the first spit to reach the brass receptacle. His words sprayed across the room. "Shoot, I thought we were still cowboys."

"You ever heard of the Day-Lyte Club?" Shorty asked.

"I think it's over there next to Earl's Auto Paint Shop on Route 66 and Wyoming Boulevard," Granddaddy offered.

When Quirt Payton shoved his revolver back into his holster, I did the same. My shirt felt drier and I placed my straw hat, crown down, on the table.

Coosie nodded at me. "Pop, you got yourself a genuine cowboy there. He already knows how to take care of his sombrero. Is it alright if I buy the lad a sody?"

I watched my granddaddy's brown eyes. His leather-tough, tan face nodded. Coosie tossed a nicket across the table like it was ante for a poker game. I scooped it up and trotted across the lobby to the Coke machine in the corner. The bottle cap opener was tied with a brass chain to the wall. I shoved the cap in my pocket because I never knew when such a useful item might come in handy. I thought I could hear cryin' in the office but didn't see anyone. I tried to peek around the corner until I got embarrassed. If the clerk would have stared back at me, I would have collapsed on the spot. So, I concluded it was the radio. Those were still the days when a radio was worth listenin' to.

They have never made a better soda pop than those little Cokes in the hourglass, green bottles. I took a deep swig, then let it dribble down my throat slow as I swaggered back over to the old cowboys.

Granddaddy raised his eyebrows.

"Thank you, Mr. Harte," I blurted out.

"You're welcome, Little Brother. You got the makings of a good hand yourself. Your grand-pop would do to ride the river with any day. You listen to him. He'll keep you square. He's a fine Christian man and the best rawhide braider in this room. No one can argue with that."

Granddaddy pulled out his makings and rolled another cigarette. "Bronc, what happened to ol' Oscar after you and Charley pushed them rustled cows down to Cholla Springs?"

Bronc unfastened the cuffs on his long-sleeved, white shirt and rolled them up to reveal a tattoo of a scantily-clad, Mexican *señorita*. I tried not to stare as my face heated.

The crash sounded like a waitress dropping

dishes, but the Matador hadn't had a restaurant since 1929.

A single angry word rolled out the doorway. My chin dropped.

"Little Brother, I believe she said 'shoot,' " Quirt explained.

Bronc nodded, then leaned forward. "Charley told me to hold the cattle and he'd go help Oscar back out of the arroyo. But I told Charley that Oscar was my pard. It was up to me to get him out of there. Charley agreed."

Thad roared. "Charley always was smart, wasn't he?"

"Yep," Shorty said. "Not as smart as the professor, but smart nonetheless."

CHAPTER 13

Coosie rubbed his front teeth with his finger as if polishing them. "Did you read where the professor died last March in Dallas?"

"No. You don't say?" Granddaddy declared. "I hadn't heard that."

"The news took a few weeks to get up here," Coosie added. "It wasn't listed in the obituaries but on the Saturday ranch page, next to feeder calf prices and hog futures."

"I wonder if any of the New Mexico boys from the old days got down to his funeral?" Quirt asked.

Bronc struggled to his feet. "Other than us sittin' in this lobby, there aren't any New Mexico boys from the old days left."

"One of us should have been there to read over the professor," Quirt insisted. "Lord knows, he read over many a cowboy in his day. Other than Pop, I've never known a man who knew the Bible better."

"Where are you goin', Bronc?" Quirt asked. "If she needs help, she'll ask for it."

"Relax, lawman. I ain't cuttin' in on you. If I'm goin' to tell a long-windy story, I'll need to deposit some coffee and to refill this pot."

Shorty McGuire scooped up the deck of cards

and dealt six each to Granddaddy and himself. "You remember the professor readin' at Red Carlton's grave? Shoot, he must have read half the Old Testament that day."

"Was that the time Silo rode all the way to Tularosa to get the sheriff?" Quirt stood, pulled off his suit coat and carefully folded it, his holstered gun more visible now.

"Yep," Shorty tossed two cards into the discard pile and waited for Granddaddy to do the same. "The Circle C and the 2-Bar-T was feudin' over them tanks up in the Sacramento Mountains . . . near the Mescalero Apache Reservation. Red got killed by a ricochet bullet."

"A ricochet?" I repeated.

Shorty tugged at his drooping mustache. "They wasn't tryin' to kill us, son. They just tossed some lead our way to scare us off. But ol' Red wasn't the type to scare. He stood out in front of those tanks like John the Baptist tauntin' King Herod."

"And they killed him?" I banged my Coke bottle on the table so hard, Quirt reached for his gun.

"Like I said," Shorty continued, "they lobbed lead about fifty feet shy, but one of them must have hit some granite and skipped like a flat stone on water and hit Red in the throat. He died right then and there, before we could get to him."

I covered my neck with both hands.

"Not a one of them 2-Bar-T men that could hit a mule deer at twenty feet," Thad insisted. "They was as lousy a shootin' outfit as ever rode the range."

Coosie's chin had been nodding on his chest, but he sat right up. "Except for Blackie Freeman. He could shoot the eyes out of a bobcat at a thousand yards."

Thad Brewer nodded. "I'll grant you that. Blackie was a fine shot. But he was in a Deming hoosegow that day sleeping off a fandango."

"A fandango?" I asked.

"That's any Mexican dance, Little Brother, where cowboys were allowed to howl. And Blackie could howl with the best of them."

"Did you ever watch Blackie when he was with Pawnee Bill's Wild West Show?" Quirt asked.

Granddaddy tossed two cards into the pot, took a slow drag on the hand rolled quirley, then let the smoke waft up to the slow circlin' ceilin' fan. "I seen Blackie bust one-hundred-ninety-nine out of two-hundred glass balls at a show in Omaha back in '09. And he did it with a .45-70 high-wall, single shot-rifle."

"I heard he missed one for the crowd," Coosie reported. "If he shot them all, city folks would think it was easy."

"It wasn't a .45 bullet that he used, Pop," Quirt insisted.

"Sure it was. I know my guns." Granddaddy laid down the four of diamonds, face up.

"Oh, it was a .45 on the outside, but with a smooth-bored barrel. He handloaded shotgun shot in them brass casings."

"You don't say? It was a shotgun all along?"

"In that case, I reckon any of us could have toured with Pawnee Bill," Shorty muttered as he tossed down a nine of clubs.

"But not the other boys of the 2-Bar-T," Quirt said. "It was a fluke shot that killed Red."

CHAPTER 14

Granddaddy slapped down the jack of diamonds, then gawked over at the Coke machine. My eyes followed his as Bronc pounded on the side of the red box.

Shorty played a black seven. "The professor asked for a ceasefire while we buried Red and the 2-Bar-T boys agreed. So Silo Coursevitch snuck down the hill and rode back to the ranch for more men and ammunition while the professor read from the book of Psalms. You remember Silo?"

"He got hit by a dadgum Greyhound Bus near Merced, California, back in '49," Quirt said.

"Yeah," Shorty said. "He drove a car like he rode a horse . . . slow and aimless."

I raised my hand. "What happened at Red's burying?"

"The professor recited for over two hours. He finished Psalms, Proverbs and just kept going. Somewhere in Ezekiel he lulled them into a stupor, I surmise," Shorty said. "Anyway, by the time they looked up Silo returned with a deputy sheriff, eight more men, and plenty of bullets. They hightailed it back to the 2-Bar-T and there wasn't a disagreement over the tanks again."

Granddaddy played the ace of spades and pegged two holes on the homemade cribbage board carved out of elk antler. "Government owns them tanks now, you know."

Coosie rubbed on his shoulder like a man with a long-buried bullet. "They owned 'em then, I reckon."

"Yeah, but now they don't let the cows graze up there." Shorty played the nine of hearts. "They say them tanks is reserved for mountain sheep, but there ain't been mountain sheep in them hills since Merica Rojas brought one down on Armistice Day."

"It took him two days to roast it," Thad said.

Granddaddy laid down the jack of clubs, then crushed his smoke in the large, amber-glass ashtray. "I never did like the taste of wild sheep."

"I ain't fond of eatin' tame ones either." Shorty played another nine and pegged one hole.

Coosie licked his full, fleshy lips. "My mama could bake a fine leg of lamb ever' Easter."

The lobby grew quiet again. The ceiling fan lapped above our heads. Rain pelted the sidewalk.

I heard whispers, and when I glanced over at Bronc he was talking to the blonde lady behind the lobby counter. I couldn't make out the words but she was pulling Kleenex and shovin' 'em to her eyes like Mrs. Welton did when the army told her John, Jr. got killed in Korea.

He ambled over with a Coke in his hand and flopped down on the sofa so hard, I felt myself shoot straight up in the air a foot. He downed the soda in one gulp, then belched. "The coffee's all gone."

Quirt straightened his tie. "You took a long time figuring that out."

"I reckon she and Mr. Flat-tire had a spat."

"That was obvious before you went over there."

Bronc leaned towards me. "Little Brother, would you like to hear the rest of the story about Oscar?"

The closer he got, the larger Bronc seemed. I nodded.

The big man leaned back in the worn, leather sofa. "Like I said, Charley wasn't as smart as the professor but smart enough to let me ride up and rescue Oscar."

"How did you get him out of there?" I asked.

"I snuck up there totin' that little Winchester '92 trapper with the fifteen inch barrel. Remember that little .44? It was a beauty of a carbine."

"Whatever happened to that gun?" Quirt's shirt collar was soaked wet with sweat, but he left it buttoned.

"I pawned it one cold December in Gallup," Bronc said. "I went back two weeks later to get it out of hock and they couldn't find it."

"How's that?" Granddaddy laid down his

hand next to the jack of hearts on top of the stack, then pegged twelve holes.

"That ol' boy was about as honest as a rose petal at the north pole," Bronc grumbled. "Some Navajo grandma is probably still shootin' coyotes from the front of her hogan with it. Anyway, I had my little carbine and snuck up there next to Oscar. While we was plannin' our retreat, I'll be dadgum if them Mexicans didn't lob a stick of dynamite over the boulders at us."

"Live dynamite?" I gasped.

"Yes sir, Little Brother. That fuse hissed like a rattlesnake in spring."

Shorty pegged six holes then turned over the kitty and shook his head. "Is that how Oscar lost his fingers?"

"Just wait," Bronc roared. "Just wait until I get there."

CHAPTER 15

The tap of high heels on the linoleum lobby floor hushed the conversation and turned heads. The blonde bookkeeper marched towards us, packing the vase of mixed spring flowers.

Six old men and one boy sprang up. Granddaddy nudged me and I yanked off my hat, like the others.

"Howdy, Miss Diane," Quirt said.

"You get the flowers today, boys." She slammed them down on the table so hard I was afraid the blue porcelain vase would break.

"Weren't them for you?" Thad asked.

Her eyes teared and voice quivered. "The jerk sent me flowers, then told me he needed more freedom. Said he wouldn't be around for a while. I don't need this."

Coosie pulled out his half-chewed cigar. "Darlin', we visited with that fella. It's our opinion that you can do better."

Shorty stood a few inches under Miss Anderson. "You're way too purdy to ride the range with a rookie like him. No ma'am, we was glad to see him ride off."

She managed a weak, but wide smile. "Thank you. Today I can use all the flattery I can get."

"That ain't flattery, ma'am," Bronc insisted.

"Flattery is lyin' in order to get something the other don't rightly want to give."

"And sayin' you are a purdy lady is just statin' a fact," Thad murmured. "No other motive than that."

"Do you want us to haul that ol' boy out behind the woodshed and school him a little?" Quirt asked.

She bit her lip, then sighed. "Thanks for the offer. I'll ponder it. It's nice to have someone on my side."

"Us at the Matador is family," Bronc insisted. "We take care of each other."

"Yep, we're like older brothers," Thad offered.

"Much older," Coosie hooted.

"Some days I think I was born a generation too late," she replied. "Where are the cowboys like you men today?"

"We're schoolin' up Little Brother," Quirt offered. " 'Course, you might have to wait a few years for him to graduate."

She stared at me until my face was as red as my hat. "I might do that. I just want someone to treat me like I'm special."

Quirt Payton rolled the brim of his hat as he rocked back on the heels of his boots. "Miss Diane, if we were forty years younger, we'd be fightin' out in the muddy street just for the right to ask you to the dance."

I stared up at Granddaddy.

Coosie came to my rescue. "Except for Pop. He's the marryin' type. He and his Katie go way back."

I couldn't help but grin in relief.

"What did that two-bit hombre tell you?" Shorty asked.

"He said it was getting too intense, that I'm too demanding."

"What were you demanding, darlin'?" Quirt quizzed.

She stared down at her feet. "That we wait until we're married."

"Good for you, Miss Diane," Granddaddy encouraged. "No one ever regretted doin' things the Lord's way."

"So he walked out on you?" Quirt pressed.

"He said he needed some time to think things through." She turned and stared at the front door.

"Sounds like walkin' out to me," Bronc challenged.

"Me too," she said. "I might have something to add to his thoughts. Where do you think he went to think things through?"

"To the Day-Lyte Club over on Highway 66 and Wyoming Boulevard," I blurted out.

She leaned down towards me. I smelled the sweetest perfume in the world. You know, kind of like layin' your head in a pillow of rose petals on a mild June day.

"What?" she pressed. Even her breath was sweet.

I fell in love for the first time, if you don't count the round-faced, brown-eyed girl in kindergarten. I swallowed hard. "He said that he . . ."

Granddaddy covered my mouth with tobacco-scented fingers.

Quirt cleared his throat. "Miss Diane, good old Leon bragged to us that he had a big date with some gal named Teresa, a dancer at the Day-Lyte Club."

"Crap!" Diane bit her lip to hold back tears. She turned away towards the registration counter.

My chin must have dropped to my lap. Up to that point, I had never heard such a word come from a lady's mouth.

"If we, perchance, meet up with him," Bronc called out. "What about the woodshed?"

"You have my permission to give the creep what he deserves." She marched past the counter and disappeared into the back room.

We all sat back down except for Quirt Payton, who trailed after Diane Anderson.

CHAPTER 16

The large bouquet of pink carnations, white daisies, blue iris, and yellow daffodils overshadowed the table strewn with cribbage boards and numberless cards. It reminded me of one of them arrangements that out-of-town folks send to a funeral to try and make up for the fact they haven't seen the deceased in years. The old cowboys gawked at it for a while and I wondered whether they were thinking about the past or the future.

Thad Brewer scooted his large frame to the front of the sofa, then reached over and plucked a white flower out of the bouquet. "Do you reckon we left 'em cryin' and didn't even know it?"

"Sometimes we knew it," Bronc replied.

"Cowboyin' ain't much of a lifestyle for a wife. It surely don't pay enough to sit you up nice," Coosie declared. "Unless a man is a good carpenter like Pop, a cowhand's better off alone."

"No one, and I mean no one," Thad grumbled, "is better off alone."

Other than Coosie's deep cough that rattled in his chest, the room quieted down like heavy clouds right before a rain.

"What I would like to know," Shorty finally

piped up, "is how can a man afford custom hats and boots . . . and a '53 Mercury . . ."

Bronc grinned. "Almost-new."

"A '53, almost-new Mercury, on a dollar-an-hour job at the filling station?" Shorty challenged.

"What are you sayin'?" Coosie asked.

"He's goin' broke or he's dippin' his glove in the company cashbox."

"You boys could be too harsh," Granddaddy scolded. "Maybe a rich father bought him the car. Or some ol' maid aunt in Tulsa willed it to him."

"I had me an almost-new 1923 Model T roadster once," Thad said. " 'Course, I didn't have it long."

"Was that the one you and your brothers took to Mexico?" Coosie asked. "C. L. told me about it."

Thad nodded. "Yep, that's it. Me and my brothers, C.L. and Ben, saved up five hundred dollars between us. Shoot, it took us a couple years to salt away that much. We bought that rig in Douglas and headed across the border. Arturo Sanchez was claimin' to be a general and raisin' Hades down near Hermosillo. The Federales were chasin' him with automobiles and he was havin' a tough time stayin' ahead of them. We heard he was wantin' to buy an automobile."

"I rode a fall gather down on the Big Bend of the Rio Grande with Arturo. He was a wild eighteen-year-old buck, but my, how he could ride," Coosie said. "And his mama is the lady that taught me to make tortillas."

"I heard you traded for some horses," Granddaddy plucked up the last peppermint on the table and dropped it into my hand.

Thad sat back on the sofa, his hands once again resting on top of his massive stomach. "It sounded good. We were goin' to trade that automobile for a hundred head of vaquero-broke mustangs, then drive them north across the border and sell them for a hundred dollars each. Ben had been lamed up since he got back from the war, and finally felt strong enough to do something besides lay around the bunkhouse. So we decided to make us some big money. Shoot, boys, if we sold them ponies for ten bucks a head, we could double our money."

Granddaddy stuffed the tiny butt of his cigarette into the glass ashtray that proclaimed in faded purple ink: New Mexico's Premier Hotel. "It didn't work out?"

"We found General Arturo Sanchez and made the trade. The horses were weaker than promised. They had been rode hard and broke down. But we babied them, lettin' them fatten up on open range before we reached the border."

"Did you use that meadow in the Sierra Madres near Dos Aquicias?" Shorty asked.

"Stayed several days," Thad reported. "It's beautiful in them hills. If there had been a cabin and a *señorita*, I'd still be there today." He noticed me staring at him. "I'd need her to cook, son. We ain't all good cooks like ol' Coosie."

"The first time I was in Dos Aquicias was with DelNorte," Coosie said. "You boys are probably too young to have met DelNorte."

"Was he as good as his legends?" Bronc asked.

"Better. Pete Mosquito was in Tucson when he heard that DelNorte had left El Paso lookin' for him. Ol' Pete turned himself in to the U.S. marshal in Prescott. He said if DelNorte was on his trail he would either end up dead or in jail. He figured to take the better option while he had a choice. Word that DelNorte was on an outlaw's trail sent most of them to South America. Any-way, he needed a posse to ride into the Madres, so he hired me and the wagon to go along and cook. We weren't there long. But that's another story."

"So, Thad, what happened to your fine Mexican horses?" Granddaddy asked.

Thad picked at the hair in his ear as if he could pull it out. "The night before we crossed back into the States, I held the horses while Ben and C.L. checked out the cantinas at Agua Prieta. Neither of them could hold his mescal, and they must have bragged a bit."

"Handsome Dave got killed in Agua Prieta, twice," Shorty mentioned. "But that's an old story."

My eyes widened, but the anecdote was dropped.

"Did the banditos show up to take the horses?" Bronc asked.

"Nope. By daylight, two hundred dadgum Federales surrounded us."

"On the border?" Granddaddy questioned.

"Don't that beat all? It was as if they had been tipped off. They called us horse thieves and demanded to see a receipt for the band of mustangs."

"You didn't have a receipt, did you?" Shorty asked.

"Yep. We was doin' it all proper, boys."

Coosie hooted. "Don't tell me you showed it to them."

"I told you, Ben wasn't feelin' too good. His head was throbbin' from too much mescal. He just wasn't thinkin' straight. So he shoved the receipt at him. 'Look here,' he bragged. 'It's signed by none other than General Arturo Sanchez.' As if on signal, all two-hundred of them uniformed farmboys pointed those ol' .45-70 single-shots at us. Since those horses had belonged to Sanchez, we were accused of aiding the enemy. We tried to explain that we didn't know right from wrong in Mexican politics. We just wanted to buy some horses."

"That must have impressed them," Granddaddy said.

"Oh, they were impressed, alright." Thad brushed his shaggy, gray hair behind his ear. "They threatened to shoot us right then and there."

I reached for my cap gun. "Was there a gun-fight?"

Thad shook his head. "Nope, son. Two hundred against three ain't a fight; it's a massacre. A man has to know when he can't win. After tyin' us to a palo verde tree most of the day, they let us loose and we crossed the border, carryin' our saddles. That's all we got. Yes, sir, I had me an almost-new automobile one time."

CHAPTER 17

Quirt Payton sauntered from the back room and plopped down on the leather sofa next to Shorty McGuire. His wire-framed glasses perched on the end of his nose like a doctor about to give his prognosis.

"How's Miss Diane?" Coosie asked.

Quirt unfastened his charcoal-gray vest. "She's takin' it hard. She's a sweet gal. Lost her husband in Korea three years ago. Said she hadn't dated since. She thought Leon was the one."

"Nice of you to look after the young widow," Bronc commented.

Quirt's hand dropped to his gun. "What do you mean by that?"

Bronc stiffened up. "I mean you are sniffin' around like a geldin' that was cut late in life."

"I can assure you, I have never been cut," Quirt sneered.

Coosie slipped his teeth into his mouth. "Boys, we must be dreamin' if we are goin' to get in a fight over a woman. But it does feel good to get the blood stirred up. Ain't much to get riled over anymore besides politics and the New York Yankees."

"Now, don't you go mentionin' them d...." Shorty glanced down at me, "eh, them dadgum

Yankees. The Cardinals is twice the team they are and you know it."

"I thought we agreed not to talk about politics and baseball, at least when Shorty is around," Thad said.

Quirt pulled a white flower from the sprawling bouquet. "What do you think we should do about Leon Daisy-giver Herbert?"

"Let's mount us some. fine ponies, ride right into the dance floor of the Day-Lyte Club . . . shoot it up . . . rope him and drag him all the way to Santa Fe . . . ," Bronc suggested.

I grabbed my hat off the table and shoved it on my head. "Can I come with you?"

"Little Brother," Granddaddy said, "you're the only one in the room that could throw his leg over a saddle. The boys are joshin'."

"We can give him a what for, if he comes back here," Shorty proposed. "But I don't reckon we'll see him again."

"We could load up in Pop's '49 Plymouth and go to the Day-Lyte Club," Bronc suggested.

"Can I go, Granddaddy?" I pleaded.

"Your grandma would die, Little Brother, if she knew I hauled you into a joint like that. We aren't going nowhere."

"Ain't that the truth," Quirt sighed. "Ain't that the truth."

There is a quiet buzz from old-time ceiling fans, like six thousand crickets, all out of tune.

People don't even notice it, until there is silence.

Right about then, I heard the fan.

We all flinched when the front door banged open. A man wearin' khaki, work pants and a long-sleeved, khaki shirt strolled in. He headed straight towards us. Following Quirt's lead, my hand went to the plastic grips of my cap pistol.

"Oh, good . . ." he said. "I see the Spring Renaissance Number 10 arrived as scheduled."

"Are you talkin' about them flowers?" Shorty asked.

"Yes. We had some mix-up with substitute delivery men this morning and I was just checking to see if everything went okay. Our regular man called in sick, had a horrible sore throat, I could barely hear him. He sent his brother-in-law to fill in. I wasn't too sure of his ability."

"Oh, they arrived on schedule." Quirt eased his hand off the old Colt.

"That's all I need to know. I feel much relieved." The man with the dark-brown, butch haircut spun on his heels and marched back out the door.

CHAPTER 18

"I don't like it," Quirt announced.

"What are you worried about now, Marshal Payton?" Granddaddy asked.

"That substitute delivery man," Quirt mumbled, "what if he just came in here to preview the place? How do we know who he was? He could be sizin' us up, that's all I'm sayin'. Like a lead man on a bank job."

"I ain't never seen a man as worried about his health as you," Bronc roared.

"I wintered at a line shack with Tuberculosis Kimbell up in the Sangre de Cristos. Now, there was a man worried about his health," Coosie said.

"Is he still at the Old Soldier's Home in Santa Monica?" Granddaddy asked.

Coosie chuckled. "Yep. I get a Christmas card from him ever' year and he always says, 'Well, Pard, I probably won't make it until next year.' "

"Payton makes me as nervous as a reverend in a dance hall, grabbin' that pistol all day long," Bronc said. "There ain't that many outlaws imprisoned in the entire state of New Mexico."

"You don't have to be here if you don't want to," Quirt snapped.

Bronc's eyes narrowed. "You'd be safer if you

69

stayed in your room and let the rest of us relax."

Thad cleared his throat. "If you two will settle down, Bronc still ain't told us how Oscar lost his fingers."

"Did he start that tale yesterday or was it today?" Coosie guffawed.

Quirt rapped on the table. "And I say, that flower delivery man was spyin' on us. My stomach is startin' to churn, boys."

Bronc ignored Quirt. "If you promise not to distract me, I'll finish up. Where was I?"

"Them Mexicans had throwed dynamite at you," Granddaddy said.

"And Charley held the cows in the draw," I added.

Bronc waved his arms like he was chasing away turkeys. "Okay, we gawked at the sizzlin' fuse, then looked at each other. Oscar fired off a round at the rocks and I leapt out as fast as I could, grabbed it up, and tossed it back at 'em. Two seconds later that same stick came flyin' back at us." Bronc waved his arms as he talked.

"Was that when Oscar lost his fingers?" I asked.

Bronc's brown eyes twinkled. "Nope, son. I'm here to say, I dove out there, yanked the fuse and cap out and tossed them behind a boulder. You know how loud them blastin' caps is. But it don't do no damage behind a rock."

"So Oscar didn't have his hand blown up, after all?" Thad pressed.

Bronc leaned back, his fingers laced behind his head. "You goin' to let me finish?"

"I'm an old man," Coosie Harte roared. "I'm hopin' to live long enough to get through this story."

A sly grin swept Bronc's leather-tough face. He sat up and leaned forward. "Okay, me and Oscar started backpeddlin' down the hill, when two half-sticks of dynamite come droppin' out of the blue sky like ducks shot with an eight gauge shotgun. They must have had a limited supply and decided half-sticks were more effective."

"So that's how he lost his fingers?" Granddaddy asked.

"Nope. We was wantin' to boot out that nest of rustlers, so we tossed them right back. They was long of fuse."

"This sounds more like a football game, than a gunfight," Shorty hooted. "They must had fuses like a kite tail."

"Little Brother," Granddaddy explained. "Those who don't know much about dynamite always make the fuse too long."

"Speedy Cay Belton used to set the shortest fuses I ever saw in my life. Did I ever tell you about the time him and me blew the ceilin' off that stone outhouse behind the Pyramid Hotel in Shakespeare?" Shorty said.

"You told us a dozen times," Thad roared.

"I thought the hotel was in Lincoln," Quirt added.

Granddaddy slapped his knee. "It was in Soccoro last time I heard."

The little man with the droopin' mustache stiffened his shoulders. "Never mind, then. I just thought Little Brother might enjoy the story."

"Let Bronc finish his, or I'll never get back to Johnny Appleseed and the Buckskin stallion," Coosie insisted.

When the two-tone, brown-and-white 1953 Pontiac backfired out on the street, all the old men flinched. Only Quirt Payton jumped to his feet, Colt drawn and cocked.

"Someday that gun will go off," Bronc groused.

"It will fire only when I want it to." Quirt plopped back down in the chair. His stare pinned me to the back of the couch. "And today just might be the day."

I felt cold sweat bead on my forehead as he eased the hammer down, and slipped the gun back into his holster.

CHAPTER 19

Conversation halted as Diane Anderson marched across the lobby. Her dark, wool skirt hugged tight against her hips and long legs.

The old men and me stood again.

"Boys, if Mr. Johnson comes in, tell him I had to take care of some important personal business. I'll be back in an hour. Emily is running the desk, but she's in back with the laundry."

"He ain't worth much effort, Miss Diane," Quirt insisted.

She rubbed her narrow chin. "Perhaps not. But it's killing me to know what this Teresa looks like."

"You want us to go with you?" Quirt rested his hand on his holstered pistol.

Miss Diane stepped up and hugged the old lawman's shoulder. A smile crept across her bright red lipstick-covered lips. "If I go riding in with a posse, there will be bloodshed," she said. "And, right now, I don't know who I want you to shoot yet. How about me taking a rain check? Thanks, boys . . . you are swell to me. Really swell."

No one sat down until she pushed out onto the sidewalk, her unopened umbrella resting on her shoulder.

"I don't think I want to be Leon Herbert when she catches up with him," Shorty remarked.

"Miss Diane will do alright. She's got spunk and sand," Quirt said. "Little Brother, find yourself a gal with spunk and sand. She won't quit on you when the hard times come."

"Yep, them others don't have a chance against the likes of Miss Diane," Coosie added.

"Unless they have dynamite," I blurted out.

Bronc laughed as we all sat back down. "That's right, son. Dynamite tends to equalize things. It's hard to believe, but them Mexicans tossed the dynamite back. I yanked the fuse and cap out of one of them half-sticks and tossed it behind the rock. But poor ol' Oscar . . ."

"The dynamite blew up on him?" I inserted.

"Nope. He yanked the fuse and cap out of his. But, bein' in a hurry, he made the mistake of tossin' the now harmless dynamite behind the rock and kept the blastin' cap and live fuse in his hand."

"A blastin' cap took his fingers off?" I asked.

"I'm here to say it did. He let out a whoop and wrapped his hand in a bandanna. Well, them Mexicans used the diversion to mount up and ride south. I looked for Oscar's fingers, but there was nothin' left of them but bits and pieces."

I grabbed my mouth. Granddaddy shoved my head down between my knees until I could catch my breath.

Bronc never missed a beat. "Oscar claimed it didn't hurt all that much, but before we had the cows moved to level ground, he passed out. Charley held the cows at the bottom of the mountains, and I rode him down to Doc Mashburn."

"In Tombstone?" Shorty asked. "Tall Doc?"

"Yep, Mashburn was working in his garden when we rode up."

Coosie licked his full lips. "The doc could really grow tomatoes. I used to sit in the shade of that woodshed of his and eat tomatoes like they was apples in October while he told tales of the Spanish War down in Cuba."

"I had never heard of this cure," Bronc continued, "but Doc had Oscar jam his hand in a pan of Tennessee whiskey."

Thad snorted. "That seems like a waste."

"Doc Mashburn had some funny ways," Granddaddy said. "He claimed a raw garlic poultice would remove warts if you left it there thirty days, but I never knew anyone who wanted to try it."

Coosie shuffled a deck of cards on the table in front of him. "Tall Doc wasn't a real doctor."

Shorty jumped to his feet. "He wasn't?"

"Nope," Coosie explained. "He had been an orderly down in Cuba during the war. Came back and couldn't get a ranch job 'cause all them soldier boys was lookin' for work, too. So he faked being a doctor."

Shorty held his right side. "But he took my appendix out one March."

"How do you know that he took it out?" Thad pressed.

Shorty paced around the table. "But, I lived through it!"

Granddaddy cut the deck. "That's as good as any real doc could have done."

CHAPTER 20

When the bell above the front door rang, two young men in jeans and white T-shirts sauntered into the lobby of the Matador Hotel. They paused, lit up cigarettes, then ambled towards us.

"Have any of you old men seen Leon Herbert?" the light-haired one said.

Granddaddy's hand slipped over my mouth.

"What's he look like?" Coosie asked.

The dark-haired one ignored looking at the men. He surveyed the room as he spoke. "Cowboy hat, mustache, yella hair, kind of thin."

"I knew a man like that down in Cruces," Thad offered.

"He had a sister named Evangeline, didn't he?" Quirt said.

Thad folded his arms, then studied the ceiling. "Don't reckon I ever heard her real name."

"Is she the one we called Sweet Pea?" Shorty quizzed.

"No, Sweet Pea's name was Evie . . ." Quirt said. "She had a birthmark on her left cheek."

"Where?" Bronc roared.

"On her face," Quirt replied.

The men in T-shirts stormed around the lobby. "Leon's here in town. He's not at the filling station. We heard he might be over here at this run-down ol' hotel."

Quirt studied their faces. "You pals of his, I reckon?" He turned and shielded his hand, but I knew he clutched the grips of his revolver.

The two gave each other a look. "Oh, we're pals, alright."

The taller one pointed to an empty couch. "Maybe we should just wait for him here."

Granddaddy scooped up the deck of cards and accordioned them from one hand to the other. "You boys play cribbage? We were about to play. Penny-a-point, of course. We could always use some new money."

The light-haired one tugged at the other. "We ain't playin' penny-ante with a bunch of old men. We'll be back for Leon."

"If he does come in, do you want us to say you were lookin' for him?" Quirt asked.

"It don't matter what you tell him. We'll find him," the darker one grumbled.

"Do you want us to give him your names?" Coosie asked.

The shorter one jabbed the taller one in the ribs. "Oh, he knows our names. That's a fact."

Bright sunlight poked through the clouds as they strutted back outside.

"Why didn't you tell them about Leon going over to the Day-Lyte Club?" I asked.

Granddaddy slipped his arm around my

shoulder. "Little Brother, a man don't jump into the stream until you see which way the water's flowin'."

CHAPTER 21

Bronc pulled a pouch of RedMan's from his back pocket and slowly unrolled it. "Penny-ante with old men, huh? I reckon that's on the mark."

Quirt Payton shuffled a deck of cards, then dealt six to Bronc and six to himself.

Bronc shoved the open pouch towards me. "Do you chew?" he grinned.

I felt my chin drop as I shook my head back and forth.

"Good. It's a nasty habit, Little Brother. You could end up lookin' like Coosie, there. Now that's a frightenin' thought."

"I ain't chewed on anything but cigars since I got these false teeth," Coosie insisted.

"In my younger days, I once got a whole block of tobaccy from none other than Stuart Brannon," Thad Brewer reported.

"Brannon didn't chew or smoke or drink," Coosie said.

"An old Ute Indian wearin' a red shirt bought a horse from Brannon. Part of the barter was a block of tobaccy, and Brannon gave it to me." Thad Brewer kept an expectant eye on the front door of the hotel. "That's the way he was, givin' stuff away."

"Brannon was the toughest sober man I ever

knew," Quirt added. "He might have been an old man when I met him, but I never saw him flinch."

Shorty McGuire put his bony hand on my knee. "Flinchin' is a weakness, boy. Don't ever develop the habit of flinchin'. Most the men buried in boot hill were flinchers."

Granddaddy winked at me. "Little Brother probably won't have to worry about flinching in a gun- fight."

"No sir, I can tell that," Shorty added. "I can see by the way he packs those pistols that he ain't the flinchin' type."

"I'll tell you another time a man shouldn't flinch . . ." Coosie continued. "That's when he's playin' cards."

Thad grinned. "Unless he's just playin' penny-ante cribbage."

"Were them boys tryin' to insult us?" Bronc said.

"I reckon. You know, I played for a few, big poker hands in my day," Quirt said. "Me and Pete Black played one hand for the entire reward for bringing in Ranky NoShoes."

"How much was that, Quirt?" Grandpa asked.

"One thousand cash dollars in twenty-dollar double-eagles back before the ol' man took us off the gold-exchange standard durin' the Depression."

Granddaddy leaned over until I could smell

peppermint and tobacco on his breath. "He means Mr. Roosevelt, Little Brother."

"I played for fifty head of Texas longhorns up in the Judith Basin of Montana back in '96," Coosie said.

"How much were they worth, Mr. Harte?" I probed.

"Anywhere from one-hundred-fifty dollars to fifteen-hundred dollars, dependin' on the year," he replied. "I always figured if I had won and let them fatten up, I could of driven them up to Alberta and made twelve-hundred dollars. I was holdin' jacks and tens. I surmised there was no way to beat me, but July Johnson was setting there with the apocalypse."

"He beat you with three sixes?" I stammered.

"I see Katie's been readin' Little Brother the Bible," Quirt said. "She's a good woman, Pop."

"Too good for an old cowhand," Thad teased.

"You won't get an argument from me," Grandpa replied. "The day Katie Hall said she would marry me was the best hand I ever drew."

"Six-six-six is the Devil's number," I added.

"I reckon it is, Little Brother. I heard say that them cows stampeded on July Johnson down on the Mussleshell and he busted his arm trying to round them back up."

"I think the biggest hand I ever played was for Liddy Chavez down in Juarez," Shorty blurted out.

"Now that was a big hand!" Bronc hooted. "Liddy must have been six-feet-tall and sturdy, if you know what I mean."

"You gambled for a woman?" I wheezed.

"We wasn't gamblin' for her . . . but for her affections," Shorty explained. "Me and The Other John Hardin, that is. We didn't figure it was worth pulling guns over, so we played one hand of seven card draw. One would get Liddy, and the other had to leave town."

"Did you lose or win, Mr. McGuire?" I asked.

"I rode out of town that night all alone," Shorty reported.

"Hah!" Thad snorted, "you didn't answer Little Brother's question. Did the winner get Liddy . . . or the loser?"

"I never was lucky with women," Shorty mumbled.

"You wasn't lucky?" Bronc roared. "One time I was up in Lake City at a . . ."

The five other men all stared right at me.

Bronc coughed and rubbed his full, fleshy lips. "Yeah, well, I reckon you all heard that one. No reason to bore you." Then he glanced over at Granddaddy. "Sorry, Pop," he muttered.

Granddaddy nodded.

Without a flinch.

CHAPTER 22

A white, long-haired cat peeked between the railings of the staircase. I followed it with my eyes as the feline meandered down a few steps.

"That's Miss Abernathy from Room 303," Quirt explained.

"The cat has her own room?" I asked.

Thad Brewer chuckled. "Yep, it's registered in her name. Of course, her maidservant, Mrs. Roseberg, lives with her."

"But neither of them come out much, at least not in the daytime," Shorty said.

"Did you boys ever consider that we have a nice widow lady like Mrs. Roseberg livin' right here at the Matador, and we haven't said ten words to her in the three years she's been here?" Quirt challenged.

"I never could trust a woman who sported a better mustache than me," Bronc said.

I glanced back up the stairs. The cat was gone. I hoped to see the mysterious, mustached lady. The ringing of the front door silenced the men in the lobby. Quirt's hand slipped down to his holstered revolver.

A tall man in a light-brown suit, with a tugged-down dark tie and the top button of his white shirt unfastened, strolled to the counter and tapped on the bell.

Shorty jumped up and slapped his bootheels on the hardwood floor as he scooted across the lobby. "No one is at the desk right now, partner. Miss Emily is in the back room. If you want to check in, I'll go fetch her for you."

The man turned to face Shorty and the others, then pulled a small notepad from his coat pocket. Rainwater spotted his coat. He pulled off his hat and laid it, brim down, on the counter. "I'm looking for a Miss Diane Anderson. I was told that she works here."

Granddaddy's hand clamped over my mouth.

"This is a hotel," Shorty let the words roll off his lips. "Lots of people come in and out of this hotel. We'll be happy to ask around for someone by that name. You a relative or a salesman?"

The man strolled across the lobby toward us.

"You boys are a protective bunch. I'm Detective Tyler Young, Albuquerque Police Department."

Quirt Payton relaxed the grip on his revolver. "You don't happen to be totin' a badge we could see, do you, detective?"

Young grinned and tugged out a brown, leather wallet, then flashed a badge. "I like your style, mister. I never mind validatin' who I am."

"We got old by being cautious," Coosie replied.

"Do you know Miss Anderson?"

"Yes, sir," Shorty said. "Why do you need to talk to her?"

"I'm investigating a robbery and shooting that took place recently."

"Miss Diane isn't a robber," Quirt declared.

"As far as I know, she's not involved. She just might know someone who is. I just want to ask her some questions. Is she here?"

"Nope," Thad replied. "It's her break time."

"Will she be back today?"

"We surmise so," Bronc said.

"What kind of robbery was it?" Granddaddy pressed.

"The Day and Night Grocery was robbed."

"Is that the Chinaman's store?" Coosie quizzed.

"Yes, three blocks over on El Rio Street. Mr. Ling Ji was shot by a couple of punks who stole all the money in the cash register and a case of Camel cigarettes."

"What's that have to do with Miss Diane?" Quirt asked.

"Right before the store was robbed, a car backed over a fire hydrant, then sped off. We think it might be connected."

"To divert attention?" Quirt said.

"Don't know that. Just want to talk to the driver."

"You think Miss Diane's the driver?" Granddaddy asked.

"People in the street witnessed a male driver,

but Mrs. Ling Ji said that a fella with slicked-back hair drove a car like that and gave Miss Anderson a lift to the store a couple times. Just tracing every lead, boys."

"Was it a '53 Mercury?" Thad asked.

The detective spun around. "How did you know that?"

"And I reckon the coupe was Dutch-cream white and wheat-harvest gold?"

"What do you boys know about this?"

"Nothing about a store robbery," Coosie reported. "But a man came in here a hour or so ago to talk to Miss Diane and he bragged about his almost-new '53 Mercury."

"Did they leave together?"

"Nope," Granddaddy offered. "Seems like they had dated some, but he was tossin' her off for some other gal. She's a nice lady, and better off without him, if you catch my drift."

"Did he give you his name?" the detective asked.

"He was quite proud of it," Bronc said. "Called himself Leon Herbert."

The detective scribbled in his notebook. "What did he look like?"

"Hollywood boots and hat," Grandpa explained. "A dime-store cowboy."

"Five-foot-ten, narrow, brown eyes, thin face, slumping shoulders, and a wispy, light-brown mustache," Quirt reported. "His voice had sort of an Arkansas drawl to it."

The detective stared at him. "Did you used to be a lawman?"

"Quirt Payton was the best marshal in Northern New Mexico," Thad declared. "He was a dadgum, good cowboy way before that."

"Quirt Payton?" the detective muttered.

"That's me."

"I read about you when I was a kid. I thought you died before the war."

"Now that's a rumor I don't mind perpetuatin'. If they think I'm dead, they won't come lookin' for me."

"You think good ol' Leon might be involved in the robbery?" Bronc questioned.

"Just trying to track down every lead."

"How is Mr. Ling Ji?" Granddaddy asked.

"He lost a lot of blood. It could go either way."

"We'll pray for him," Grandpa said.

"I can tell you right now, Leon didn't shoot Ling Ji," Quirt declared. "He's not the type to pull a trigger. But he is the type to run over a hydrant and let someone else pull the trigger."

The detective shoved his notebook into his suit coat pocket. "Which way did Herbert head?"

"He said he was going to the Day-Lyte Club," I piped up, then covered my mouth with my hand. "Was I suppose to wait until I saw which way the creek was flowin'?" I mumbled.

Coosie rubbed his bald head. "I reckon the creek's already flowin' this time, Little Brother."

"Do you know if Herbert is carrying a weapon?" the detective asked.

"No gun," Bronc replied. "But who knows what's in those fancy boots?"

"You figure he's the type to pull a knife?"

"He might pull it," Bronc declared, "but he'll throw it down and run at the first sign of trouble."

"Unlike them other two," Shorty declared.

"What other two?" the detective pressed.

CHAPTER 23

Quirt Payton spent ten minutes with Detective Tyler Young near the front door of the lobby. When he returned, Granddaddy and Shorty were playing cribbage, as were Thad Brewer and Bronc. Coosie dealt me a hand but I failed to draw a double-run and had only a pair of tens to peg, so I didn't mind the interruption.

"There have been a string of robberies from Wyoming Street to San Mateo, along Route 66 and over by the Fairgrounds."

"I ain't read nothin' about them," Coosie said.

"It's been kept quiet 'cause the thieves threatened to harm family members if any of the shopkeepers talked to the police."

"Nice fellas."

"Two-bit punks," Bronc growled.

"These two are stealing more than quarters. Several thousand has been taken, according to Detective Young," Quirt said. "Some got stabbed. These boys are half-crazy."

"Pop, you ran a store down in Lordsburg. Did you ever get robbed?" Shorty asked.

"Only once . . . I cold-cocked him with my Colt and tied him up with clothesline. I reckon wearin' a gun on my hip all the time dissuaded them a tad. It was durin' the Depression and Katie was feedin' that ol' boy a baloney sandwich, cookies and milk by the time the sheriff showed up. She invited him over for supper when he got out of jail."

"I reckon he was just a hungry hobo," Coosie said.

"We still get a Christmas card from him."

"But nowadays they are mean," Thad Brewer added. "They don't just want some food or money, they want to hurt someone."

"Did you ever run across Cutty Swearingen?" Quirt asked. "He was crazy like that. He tried to cut your face or neck to show off his handiwork."

"The only time I faced Cutty was in Las Cruces on January 1st, double-ought. You remember all the wild things that happened then?" Bronc probed. "Ol' Cutty came diving across the big dance hall above the feed store."

"Double-ought was 1900, son," Granddaddy whispered.

"He claimed I insulted his girl," Bronc said.

"By dancin' with her, or not dancin' with her?" Thad Brewer laughed.

"I never did know that. Shoot, boys, we was ringin' in a new century. I could have danced with the mayor's wife, for all I know. I stepped out of the way the first time he lunged, and on the way past, I slammed my fist into his face. Broke his nose. Blood spurted out like a bullet hole in a rain barrel."

I held my breath. Grandpa shoved my head between my knees again, but I sat right up.

"What happened on the second lunge?" Shorty asked.

"That one made me mad, boys. The first one was just good sport, the kind of thing that happens when the fireworks go off and ever'one is celebratin'." Bronc pounded his massive fist into the palm of his hand. "But he gathered himself up off the floor and dove at me with that double-sharpened knife."

"Did he stick you, Mr. Bronc?" I stammered.

"No, Little Brother. This time I hit him above the ear. He was out cold before he hit the dance floor. I figured his girl would come take him away, but she never revealed herself. I dragged him over to the bench, dipped a towel in the punch, shoved it against his face and went on dancing. They say he didn't wake up until noon the next day."

"That's a long time to be passed out," I said.

Bronc grinned. "It was a good punch, Little Brother."

"I reckon there have always been idiots with a knife or gun," Shorty said. "The best way to stop 'em is to never let them pull that knife in the first place."

"That's right," Quirt Payton said. "You pin a knife man's shoulders to the wall and he can't reach his boot . . . or the back of his duckin's."

"I saw a picture of Jim Bridger in a book and he had his knife right on his belt, up front so everyone could see," I offered.

"They called him Ol' Gabe 'cause he'd suddenly appear an' help them out of a tight spot, just like the angel of Gabriel. He was a good man, so I hear," Coosie said. "He died north of here when I was a little younger than you. He had some Mexican relatives that sold me a fine, black stallion."

"Is that the one that ran off with the wild horses?" Shorty asked.

Coosie pulled his half-chewed cigar out of his mouth. "No, that was a pinto that I traded a frying pan full of trout for."

"You traded a frying pan for a horse?" I asked.

"Not just a pan, Little Brother," Coosie flashed his toothless smile. "It was a pan full of fish."

"That doesn't seem like a good trade," I said.

"Never trade when you're hungry, Little Brother," Granddaddy cautioned.

"Didn't you feel guilty getting a horse for some fish?" I asked.

"Nope, that night the horse ran off and joined a wild band up in the Sangre de Cristos. For years I missed havin' that fryin' pan," Coosie chuckled.

"I never worry about the man that carries his knife out for all to see. He's sayin' 'let me alone, or I'll fight back' and that's fair enough," Quirt explained. "The dangerous ones are those that hide their knives. They'll sneak up and stab a man in the back."

"That's what happened to Log McDonald," Shorty said. "Some sneakthief in Silver City knifed him in the back when at the chuck-a-luck table."

"No one in his right mind would play chuck-a-luck. The house always wins," Thad insisted.

"Of course, sometime you don't know where a knife is hidin'," Shorty piped up. "Bertha down at Cactus Ranch Saloon in El Paso used to hide her knife in her . . ."

Grandpa cleared his throat.

Shorty glanced at my wide eyes. "In her purse, Little Brother. Bertha hid her knife in her purse."

"You figure things are getting excitin' over at the Day-Lyte Club about now?" Coosie asked.

"Let's see . . . Leon goes after the dancer, Teresa . . . Miss Diane goes after Leon . . . the store thieves go after Leon . . . then Detective Young goes after the thieves," Bronc mused. "Yep, I reckon we haven't had that much excitement since the mouse ran up Coosie's pants leg with the lobby full of ladies from the Sunday School Convention."

"There's a scene I would rather not recall," Coosie said. "When I get to them pearly gates, I trust one of them ladies don't have guard duty."

"You surmise that we will get to see them pearly gates?" Thad asked.

"According to Pop, that's more up to Jesus than to us," Quirt mumbled.

"I told you boys," Granddaddy explained, "it ain't what you did, but what He did that matters. All you got to do is believe it."

"You goin' to preach at us again, Pop?" Bronc asked.

"I'm not goin' to stop until we are all playin' cribbage together in heaven."

I looked up at my granddaddy. "Are there going to be playing cards in heaven?"

He winked. "Yep, Little Brother, I believe there will be. But don't tell your grandma or she'll get the women organized against it."

Quirt Payton stood and ambled across the lobby. "It's stopped rainin'. Maybe we should go for a stroll."

"The sidewalk is slick," Coosie said. "I don't walk too far with these bad knees."

"Maybe a drive would be nice," Shorty added. "Pop's got a nice Plymouth sedan."

"I told you, boys, I can't take Little Brother to the Day-Lyte Club. Katie would pitch a fit, and I'd have to move in over here with Shorty or Quirt."

"I can wait in the car, Granddaddy. Please!" I begged.

He jammed his silverbelly-gray Stetson on his

head. "I suppose we could drive by the front of the joint, just to see if there's activity. Maybe we'll stop by the root beer stand on the way back."

I was surprised that it was still 1954 when I pushed out into the May cloudy day. Somehow I expected horses to be tied to the rail, instead of the dark-green, '49 Plymouth.

CHAPTER 24

Granddaddy, Quirt and Bronc piled in the front seat. That left Coosie, Thad, Shorty and me in the back. It surely must have been a humorous sight. Bronc insisted on leaving his window open so he could spit. Coosie hung over the edge and couldn't close his door, so he pushed one foot to the running board and clutched the door as tight as he could. I sat sideways sandwiched between Shorty and the door. None of us had ever heard of seatbelts back then. I fought for a breath in the midst of tobacco smoke, Old Spice and sweat.

"This ain't nothin', Little Brother. Durin' the war, ten of us rode over to Arizony in a '37 LaSalle," Bronc reported. "Shorty, you was with us, weren't ya?"

"Shoot, yeah, we took the trunk lid clean off and I sat back there," Shorty explained. "It wasn't too bad until it rained."

"I rode on the running board from Gallup to St. Johns," Bronc said. "I reckon I picked bugs out of my teeth for a week."

"When did you buy your first car, Pop?" Quirt asked.

"I bought a well-used, 1917 Model T Ford in October of 1921. I drove it to Texas to visit some of Katie's folks and it died there. I sent her home on the train and bought me a team of mules. I pulled it all the way back to New Mexico."

"Was that the one that sat out at the Circle ML for years?" Coosie asked.

"Yep, that was it. I never could get it to go over ten miles without dyin'. I sold it to Slab McFenny for twenty cash dollars, half a beef, and six quarts of cherry preserves."

"Is Slab the one who took ten goats and disappeared into the Grand Canyon?" Thad asked.

"No, that was Calburt McFenny," Granddaddy explained. "Slab pulled that car home and spent two years getting it to run."

"Did he fix it?" Coosie pressed.

"Ever'thin' but the brakes. He decided to take the missus up to Jemez Springs, but just past San Ysidro, the brakes went out. He dumped it into the river close to the pueblo."

"Did I ever tell you about the time me and Double-Nate Becklam rode wild cows out of Jemez Canyon?" Shorty blurted out.

"About once a week for the last twenty years," Bronc grumbled, then spit out the window. Coosie pulled the back door shut so he didn't catch the ricochet tobacco.

"I've never heard that story," I replied.

"Slab's wife could be rather demanding, as I recall," Quirt said.

Shorty patted my knee. "Well, Little Brother, let

me tell you ridin' a wild cow is not like ridin' a horse."

"I heard that even when they was livin' up at Chama, she made him take a bath ever' Saturday night," Coosie called out from the back seat.

I scooted towards the front, so I could breath better. "You really rode a wild cow?"

"Did Slab marry that yellow-haired school-teacher from Raton?" Thad probed.

"I surely did, son," Shorty replied. "Rode her for eight straight hours."

"McGuire, I can only hear one conversation at a time, so quit lyin' to the boy," Coosie demanded.

"It ain't a lie, Little Brother," Shorty insisted. "Jist because they ain't done it, don't mean it's a lie."

"I think Ernie Biggers married that Raton schoolteacher," Bronc declared.

"No, Ernie got killed in Cuba," Quirt reported. "It must have been Earl."

"Slab was married to one of the Setter girls from over near Taos," Granddaddy reported.

"Did you ever work cattle with ol' man Setter?" Coosie asked. "He knew his cattle but he demanded a lot from his men. Long hours and low pay."

"I ain't never had a job that wasn't like that," Thad replied.

Granddaddy eased around the corner onto Highway 66 as if he was hauling brim-full open milk cans. "I heard ol' man Setter got shot four different times by his own crew."

"That ain't so," Coosie corrected. "Three times by his own men, and once by his son-in-law."

"And he lived through them all?" I asked.

"Yep," Coosie explained. "Some men just won't die no matter what you do to them."

"Is he still alive?" I asked.

Coosie shook his head.

"How did he die?" I asked.

"I think he suffocated sitting in the back seat of a crowded automobile," Thad Brewer grumbled.

"Hey, pull over there!" Quirt pointed to city bus benches at the corner where one lady sat with her head nearly in her lap.

Granddaddy slammed on the brakes and tossed us all forward. "Why in tarnation?"

Quirt jammed on his cowboy hat, and straightened his black tie. "I said, pull over!"

Granddaddy cruised into the parking lot of a hardware store.

"Park by those bus benches," Quirt instructed.

As we approached, I surveyed the benches. "What's wrong with that lady?"

Grandpa turned off the ignition and rubbed his narrow chin. "She's upset or cryin'."

Quirt shoved Bronc out the door and scampered out after him. "That ain't just any lady. That's Miss Diane. You boys wait here, I'll go talk to her."

"We'll all go," Bronc insisted.

Quirt led the way down the sidewalk to the bus stop. "Miss Diane, are you alright?"

"I didn't want you seeing me like this; I was going to get rid of the tears before I came back to the hotel."

"Is it because of Leon?" Shorty ventured.

She nodded.

I sat down on her right side, Quirt on her left. The rest plopped down in a row until both benches were filled.

"Did you boys come looking for me?"

Bronc spit tobacco out into the street, then pulled off his floppy, cowboy hat. "We was getting a mite concerned."

"Did you find Leon with that dancer?" I asked.

She put her arm around my shoulder. "Yes, I did, so I guess I'll just have to wait for you to grow up."

I wanted to marry her right then and there, but I knew Grandma would have died of a heart attack.

"I can't believe you're all looking after me," she said.

"When them two sneakthieves came in looking for Leon . . . and later on a policeman . . . we figured you might need some help," Quirt said.

"Sneakthieves?"

Shorty's hat screwed on low and made his ears

stick out. "Didn't they show up at the Day-Lyte Club lookin' to settle a score with Leon?"

She sniffed. "I took one look at him dancing close to that woman and left. He didn't even know I spied on him. Who was looking for him?"

"Detective Tyler Young and two robbers. A couple of punks with knives and guns. We figured you was in hot water and we came to bail you," Coosie explained.

"If Leon's in some sort of trouble," Quirt said, "we didn't want you to get pinched with him."

"What sort of trouble?"

"Maybe we ought to mosey over to the Day-Lyte Club and find out. It might be educational." Thad slapped his knee.

Miss Diane took a Kleenex out of her purse and wiped her eyes. "But if there is trouble, I don't want you boys to get hurt."

Quirt opened his worn suit coat to reveal the holstered revolver. "We can take care of things. It ain't exactly the first time we faced his type."

A black-and-white patrol car pulled over to the curb. The policeman at the wheel leaned across the seat and rolled down his window. "Excuse me, ma'am, are these old men harassing you and your boy?"

She sat straight up and hugged my shoulder. "My boy? Why, this is my fiancé, and these gentlemen are my brothers."

There have been a half-dozen times when life's

blessings were so great, I could barely contain myself. This was one. I wondered how heaven could ever be better than that moment.

When Miss Diane agreed to ride with us to the Day-Lyte Club, it presented a logistical problem. We had no room for another passenger. We must have sit there ten minutes until Quirt decided that we could leave the trunk lid open, and me and Shorty could ride in the trunk. I thought it wasn't right that I didn't get to sit with the woman I was going to one day marry, but one scowl from Granddaddy sent me clamoring to the back of the Plymouth.

It was only three or four blocks to the Day-Lyte Club, but it seemed longer from the confines of that trunk.

CHAPTER 25

Folks today think that 1954 existed in some other galaxy, on some other planet. Maybe they are right. It's hard to believe that world and this one are made of the same stuff.

In 1954, Route 66 was America's highway. The interstate system lingered as an ambitious idea in the mind of President Dwight David Eisenhower. I wonder if the present generation can imagine cross-country, auto travel without freeways, fast food joints, and motel chains. Not that I'm arguing to return to the past. But it was certainly creative and colorful.

Along Route 66 in Albuquerque, motels sprouted up that looked like a string of small cottages, most centered around a Southwest theme. Each tried to outdo each other in gaudiness. Cafés, mostly mom-and-pop diners, specialized in lots of food and grease. And no matter how many tourists traveled to the Promised Land of Southern California, Highway 66 remained two lanes.

A crowded two lanes, with most folks in a hurry.

Except for the '49 Plymouth, with a lad, an open trunk, six old cowboys and Miss Diane Anderson.

The Day-Lyte Club began in 1910 with the unremarkable name of "Joe's Saloon." During Prohibition, a second story was added to the 34′ by 80′ building. The upstairs comprised one big dance hall. Downstairs was called the Slavic Social Club. In 1933, the façade was modernized and it reopened as Day's Lounge. Somewhere toward the end of the 30s, "Albuquerque Al" put in some rooms and a central bath on the upper floor. The rooms were used a lot during the war, I hear, but I'm not sure it was a real hotel. When Al moved to San Diego in 1945, the building sat vacant for a year or two. Then the Lyte brothers from El Paso moved up and restarted the business. Neon signs hung out front and glass, building-block windows lined the street side. By 1950, small bands were hard to book, and Tony Lyte decided to feature dancing girls. "Just like the 'Copa', only different," the sign read.

Some folks said they served the best steaks in town.

Others claimed it was the devil's playground.

The truth is somewhere in between, but for me, the place symbolized the mysteries of life isolated from a ten-year-old boy who would not gain access to a television set for two more years.

Granddaddy pulled into the far end of the parking lot next to the auto paint shop. No doubt he hoped that no one would drive by and recognize his Plymouth. Shorty crawled out of the trunk, then helped me. "Now, mind you, I don't want to ride to Tucumcari back there, but it wasn't too bad."

Quirt Payton organized them in the parking lot. "Coosie, you and me are the only ones got our holsters filled. So you sit at the bar nearest the front door and watch over us. Pop, you, Shorty and Thad find one table. Me and Bronc will find another. Some will suspect somethin' if we all sit together."

"What kind of trouble are we expectin'?" Thad asked.

"Quirt sees ambushes in ever' shadow," Bronc reminded them.

"I don't reckon anyone is lookin' for us, but if them two show up to settle with Leon, we'd like a ringside seat," Quirt said.

"Did I ever tell you the time I watched Joe Lewis?" Shorty remarked.

"I thought you fought Joe Lewis," Bronc roared.

Coosie laughed, too. "No, he fought Josephine Lewis down in Lincoln."

"I'd rather fight Joe Lewis than her," Shorty mumbled. "But I was there on April 17, 1939, in Los Angeles when none other that Joe Lewis himself knocked out Jack Roper in the first round."

"The best fight I ever seen was in Jerome, Arizona. Tabor Williams was fightin' Red Dutch and they went at it bare-knuckles for seventy-one rounds." Thad glanced at me. "In them days a fight wasn't over until one of them couldn't stand up."

Granddaddy rolled down the sleeves on his white shirt and buttoned the cuffs. His gray hair had a short curl under his narrow-brimmed Stetson. I knew he would be giving himself a haircut any day now. "Little Brother, you wait in the car."

I bit my lip. I knew that cowboys don't cry, but it was hard to hold it in.

"Nonsense," Miss Diane insisted. "Little Brother and I are going to sit in the front while you scout the back room for Leon and that woman."

Granddaddy shook his head. "If this ever gets to Grandma . . ."

"She won't want Little Brother to help out a lady in distress?" Miss Diane teased.

Granddaddy sighed. "Come on, Little Romeo, but I surmise I will live to regret this."

"Relax, Pop," Bronc said, "it ain't like this is the Saddle Horn in Deming."

"Nothin' is like the Saddle Horn in Deming," Quirt added. "That was the only time I ever got shot."

I gave him a quick jab. "Where did you get shot, Mr. Payton?"

"At the Saddle Horn in Deming," Quirt repeated.

"But, I meant . . ." Granddaddy's hand clamped hard on my shoulder.

"Give me your hand, Little Brother," Miss Diane said.

I don't remember much about the front door at the Day-Lyte. It must have been tall, 'cause my high-top, black tennis shoes rose ten feet off the ground when I sauntered in there, holding Miss Diane's hand.

The lounge was fogged with cigarette smoke, but I never heard anyone complain. Hollywood made cigarette smoking glamorous after the war. Most of the citizens of Albuquerque would have declared it the least dangerous activity in the Day-Lyte Club. Several dark-green, plastic booths lined the front of the building under glass block windows. A menagerie of assorted tables and chairs huddled like tourists in a plaza around an open dance floor, with a tiny bandstand at the back of the room.

Along the north side of the building was a long bar decorated with a yellowed oil painting of a black racing horse and a faded, autographed, movie poster of bare-legged Betty Grable starring in *Sweet Rosie O'Grady*.

CHAPTER 26

Miss Diane motioned for me to slide closer in the circular booth as Quirt Payton, Bronc, and Thad Brewer scooted in. Grandpa and Shorty McGuire pulled up chairs on the end.

Coosie Harte hunkered at the end of the bar as scout.

"Did we miss all the excitement?" Miss Diane asked.

"Those two store thieves came in on the prowl," Quirt reported, "but before they got settled at a table, Detective Young showed. They must have met him before because they took out the back door quicker than a pup in a skunk den."

"Did the detective follow them?" Miss Diane asked.

"According to the old boy at the bar with the yellow shirt, he didn't spot them. He looked around, then left by the front door," Shorty said.

Miss Diane half-shut her eyes. "Where were Leon and . . . that woman . . . during all this?"

"They got in a spat," Thad Brewer said.

Bronc took up the conversation. "This dancin' gal, Teresa, dropped a nickel in the jukebox and started listenin' to Hank Williams sing 'Your Cheatin' Heart.'"

"Hank can really sing, can't he?" Shorty added.

"Maybe the song was too personal," Granddaddy said. "He grabbed her hand to yank her out to the dance floor and she slapped him loud enough for the bartender to hear."

"What happened then?" I asked.

"According to the boys playin' poker over there, Leon stormed off to the men's room muttering to himself," Bronc reported.

Thad Brewer rubbed his thumbless hand. "That's when them two thieves came in lookin' for him."

"While he was in the men's room?" Quirt roared.

"That's the story," Shorty said. "When Miss Teresa spied them, she grabbed her jacket and umbrella and rushed out the front door."

Quirt kept his eye on the customers coming in the door. "By the time Leon emerged from the john, the store robbers, the detective, and Miss Teresa were gone."

"Leon tried to get near ever'one in the room to tell him what direction she left, but they all played dumb," Shorty explained.

Thad whistled. "I don't reckon that made him too happy."

"He said a few choice words not fit for woman or child," Bronc glanced over at me. "Then left, not more than ten minutes before we sauntered in."

Granddaddy pulled off his wire-framed

glasses. "It's a good thing he wasn't here when those two hoodlums marched in here."

"You never know the luck of a lousy calf," Bronc murmured.

Miss Diane fidgeted with her small, round, red earring. "I was just thinking how lucky he was to be gone when this posse of seven cowboys moseyed in."

"Six and a lad," Granddaddy corrected.

"No," she said. "Seven men."

Quirt waved his finger as if to emphasize a point, then paused and tilted his head.

The others at the booth turned back toward the dark end of the Day-Lyte Club, to stare at the jukebox while Tex Ritter sang, "Do Not Forsake Me, Oh My Darlin'."

When the song ended, Shorty shook his head. "That was a fine movie."

"Hit too close to home," Quirt mumbled.

"I heard Cooper cowboyed up in Montana," Shorty said.

"Don't know if he did or he didn't, but he grew up in Helena," Thad reported. "Boxer Quick told me he knew the family."

"Was that Big Boxer or Little Boxer?"

"Little Boxer . . . Big Boxer died in that fire at a, eh . . ." Bronc glanced over at me, "hotel in Virginia City."

"Did you ever see Big Boxer knock out two men with just one punch?" Shorty asked.

"How did he do that?" I asked.

"It was a stunt he pulled from time to time," Shorty explained.

"Big Boxer is the only man I've known who was mean when he was sober and peaceful as a kitten when he was drunk," Granddaddy said.

"People was always buying him drinks." Shorty glanced at Granddaddy as if suddenly clamped onto by a Gila monster. "You don't suppose that was all just a game to get others to buy the drinks?"

Granddaddy rubbed his clean-shaven chin. "That thought has occurred to me more than once."

"What are we goin' to do now?" Thad quizzed.

"The quicker I get Little Brother out of the Day-Lyte Club, the longer my lifespan will be," Granddaddy insisted.

Quirt pushed his hat back. "We might as well head back to the Matador."

"Can we swing by the five-and-dime?" Shorty asked. "To buy me a needle and thread. I got my shirt caught on the radiator and shot them buttons across the room like a Gatlin' gun. Little Brother, did I ever tell you the time I . . ."

"Shorty, you can tell him in the trunk," Quirt insisted. "Thad, go get Coosie. Let's get out of here before they give us supper menus."

The air was fresh when we pushed outside

the Day-Lyte Club. Fresh and damp. A soft sprinkle fell without a sound.

"I ain't gettin' in the trunk when it's rainin'," Shorty demanded.

"It's only for a few blocks. You ain't goin' to melt," Coosie said.

Miss Diane opened up her umbrella. "I'm goin' to catch the bus back to the hotel, so I don't get fired. You need to stop by Woolworth's."

I blurted out, "I can ride with you, to make sure you are safe."

"If you go with me, Little Brother, who will take care of these old men? I'll see you all back at the Matador." Miss Diane patted my shoulder, strolled across the parking lot, and hopped into the bus before we splashed our way to the Plymouth.

Once again, three straddled the front seat and four in the back. Bronc rolled his window half-way up, but those of us in the back seat still got a little rain plastering our faces.

At least, I assumed it was rain.

CHAPTER 27

The F. W. Woolworth store was downtown on Central Avenue, also known as Route 66. That's back when highways traveled through every town they passed. Even in 1954, this produced congested traffic. Although the population of Albuquerque in 1954 peaked out just over one-hundred-thousand, it seemed like the largest city on earth to me. By the end of the decade, the town would double in size and lose its old Southwest feel.

Six old cowboys and a lad fogged up windows as Granddaddy decided to circle the block and wait for a parking spot to open. "Coosie, did you ever' cowboy up in the Dakotas?" he asked.

"I drove some agency beef to Pine Ridge a couple of times. The second time I did it, I was cookin' for the XIT."

"Did you ever make it into the Black Hills? I hear it could rain for weeks and weeks in them mountains," Shorty said. "I ought to go up there some day and see ol' Borglum's statues carved in the mountains."

"I didn't go much beyond Fort Rob, Nebrasky. Some locals came out and took the herd from there. It wasn't too many years after that ruckus

at Wounded Knee and we was a little shy of rilin'
up the Sioux."

"Did you ever fight any Indians?" I asked him.

Coosie leaned forward so he could see me
over Thad and Shorty. "I fought cattle thieves
and cutthroats for over fifty years, and some of
them was Indian and most of them wasn't."

"A cattle thief is a cattle thief, Little Brother,"
Granddaddy added. "No matter what color he is."

"Them dime novels did Indians a disservice,"
Quirt added. "About all you read is the scalpin' of
women and children. Most ones I know is as
peaceful as a Sunday School teacher. They all
seem to have a great sense of humor."

"Up in the northern part of the state, them
Pueblo Indians are all pretty dadgum good
farmers," Coosie said.

"The Apaches were a handful down south,"
Bronc said. "I signed on to be Nighthawk with
Colonel Porter Anatone when he brought Mexican steers up from Chihuahua. Just a sixteen-
year-old kid, I tried to hold the horses at night.
We was in Apache country for six weeks and
ever' night they tried to steal horses. We ended
up circlin' the cows around the horses. I still
lost half the remuda by the time we made it to
Tularosa."

"Did they shoot at you with bows and arrows?"
I asked.

"The ones I saw carried Winchesters. But they

was silent and secret when they stole horses. They didn't want to wake up a dozen angry cowboys."

As we passed in front of Woolworth's again, Granddaddy mumbled something about the earth growing overpopulated because some families had too many kids. I don't remember the exact phrase, but had he said it at home, Grandma would have replied with a forceful, "Theo!"

"I got shot by an arrow one time," Shorty McGuire declared.

"You did? Where?"

"In Reserve," he replied.

"That's a town, Little Brother," Coosie explained.

I bit my lip and added, "I mean, where did the arrow hit you?"

"I had to stand in the stirrups for a long time," Shorty answered.

"An Indian shot you?"

Shorty brushed down his mustache with his fingertips. "Yep."

"Did they try to steal your horse?" I asked.

"Nope," Shorty declared. "It was a Saturday night, and I was tired of cow camp. So me and Half-a-Bill Squires rode into Reserve to clean the dust out of our throats."

Watchin' Shorty caused me to rub my soft, bare, upper lip. "Why did they call him Half-a-Bill?"

Shorty stared off into the street as if pondering a secret formula for jet fuel. "I don't know. I never asked him. Anyway, I was riding a paint horse I called Full Moon. It was crowded at the rail and we tied off back in the greasewood patch."

"That's a funny name for a horse," I interrupted.

"Now you sound like the professor," Coosie said. "He thought it was foolish to name horses. He never did name a one he rode."

Shorty cleared his throat. "We must have got served some bad mescal, because when me and Half-a-Bill left a little after midnight, we couldn't find our horses."

"Did someone steal them?" I quizzed.

"That's what we assumed." Shorty leaned over and tapped my knee. "We staggered around town in the dark lookin' for the paint horse and a red-roan. I spotted the paint out behind the Meribel's Trading Post, but without saddle and bridle and blanket. I was fightin' mad and made a ruckus untyin' the horse."

"Did you shoot anyone?" I probed.

"No, I didn't. But I started to lead the horse towards the saloon when a voice from behind the tradin' post said 'Bring the horse back or I'll shoot.' " Shorty held his hat in his hands. "I whipped around but in the shadows I couldn't see anyone. Me and the horse stood out in the full moon, but I didn't see a soul on the back porch of the tradin' post. I checked the lever of my carbine and shouted, 'This is my horse, and I'm taking him.' The female voice came back, 'It's my mare and you are not taking her.' "

"A female? You got shot by a woman?" I stammered.

"An arrow don't know no gender," he huffed. "Let me finish my story. I figured she was bluffin' when I didn't see any rifle or gun, so I turned back to lead the horse away. I got stung in the rear end like someone drove in a twenty-penny nail with a sledgehammer."

"The lady shot you with an arrow?"

"A Navaho woman that worked for Meribel."

"Mary Sixtoes?" Thad questioned.

Shorty rolled his mustache. "She's the one."

"Bug Kelly married her, didn't he?"

"Nope, he married the other Navajo that Meribel had workin' in the trading post. The one called Sara Sarah," Quirt reported.

"Anyway," Shorty continued, "by the time they got the arrow out and cauterized the wound, it was daylight."

"How did they do that?" I asked.

"By pouring whiskey on it until I stopped hollerin'."

"You hollered?"

"I kept shoutin', 'Don't waste good whiskey!' "

"You took the wrong horse, didn't you? It really was her horse."

"Yep, Half-a-Bill found ours behind the saloon still tied to the greasewood. We had been a tad disoriented. Bad mescal will do that to a fella, you know."

CHAPTER 28

When Wal-Mart was beyond anyone's imagination, we had five & dime stores like Newberry's and Woolworth's. To be honest, I don't remember when all the items were that cheap, but my mama knew 'cause she worked at Woolworth's right out of high school. Even in 1954, most of the merchandise was inexpensive. And they had everything. What a marvelous world for a boy from the country who thought the Fuller Brush man had so much merchandise in his Chevrolet CarryAll that it must surely be sinful.

To the casual observer, we must have looked like an invasion of old men in narrow-brimmed Stetsons, cowboy boots, white shirts buttoned at the collar, and a little boy with plastic cap guns holstered to his side. But to my ten-year-old imagination, we were a posse surveyin' a crowd, on the trail of some bad hombres.

Since Shorty requested the stop, he led the way.

Woolworth;s consisted of a huge, two-story, corner building, with a full basement which contained bargain and sale items. I remember getting lost down there one time when I went on a remnant shopping trip with Grandma. I feared I might never see the light of day. Five at the time, I vowed never again to go into any "Bargain

Basement." Except for buyin' a baby crib in 1964, I kept that vow.

I never did know what was upstairs. Grandpa shrugged his thin, bony shoulders and muttered, "women's stuff." But the ground floor held the lunch counter and exhibited every under-a-dollar item known to mankind. The long rows of counters and cases had walkways behind them where the clerks stalked like caged lions, bored with their location and needing little excuse to pounce.

Bronc meandered to the newspaper counter and flipped through a *Police Gazette*. Thad Brewer parked himself by the paperbacks and plucked up an Ernest Haycox novel. Grandpa studied a new razor strap, while Coosie shuffled towards the men's room. Shorty headed for the thread and needle section. That left me and Quirt Payton to saunter toward the toys.

"Did Pop ever show you his Colt .44s?" Quirt asked.

"Yes, sir. I got to shoot them on my 10th birthday, but you can't tell Grandma."

Quirt kept one eye on the front door of the dime store. "Pop is probably the best target shooter in this bunch."

I could feel my blue, gingham shirt tighten as my chest swelled.

"That is, as long as no one's shootin' back. In the old days, Little Brother, it didn't matter how

121

quick you could get your gun out of the holster, or how accurate your target practice. The best shots kept their calm in the midst of bein' shot at."

"Who is the best at that kind of shooting?" I stopped to stare at a pressed-metal, tin badge that read, U.S. Deputy Marshal.

"I reckon I've been shot at more than the others," Quint said. "But ol' Coosie never flinched when bein' shot at. He'd be my pick of a partner in a pinch. Did your grandpa ever tell you about that ruckus at Hacienda Flats?"

I chewed on my tongue as I tried to count the change in my pocket without removing it. "I don't think so."

"Me and Pop was young bucks then, but Coosie had been around. We was deputized to ride out after a horse thief named Mexican O'Kelly."

"O'Kelly doesn't sound like a Mexican name."

"He was only half-Mexican. Anyway, we thought all we had to do was tag along with Sheriff Roger Garrett and get paid two dollars a day."

"Was he the one that shot Billy the Kid?"

"Nope, that was Pat Garrett. Roger was sheriff up in Durango, Colorado, until he died in an outhouse fire, but that's a different story. Anyway, this sheriff sent Coosie, me and Pop down the south fork of Meadow Creek 'cause we was green kids and he didn't think Mexican O'Kelly had gone that way."

I picked up the flat package that contained the deputy's badge and studied the price tag. "Did you find him?"

"He found us. About noon, I wanted some coffee. So I pulled out my pot and built a little brush fire. We was catchin' a siesta in the southern Colorado noon sun and thinking about how to spend the two bucks a day we was makin', when we heard the lever check on his gun. All three of us leapt to our feet, but O'Kelly had us covered with an old '73 carbine."

I studied the old lawman with the glasses and tried to imagine him as a kid.

"O'Kelly growled, 'Lay those guns down on the dirt. I feel insulted that sendin' green kids out after me is the best Sheriff Garrett can do.' Me and your grandpa obliged quick. We was young and hadn't stared down the big bore of a .44 carbine before."

Being made of superb quality, pressed tin, the badge was not cheap: forty-nine cents. I glanced up. "Didn't Coosie lay down his gun?"

Quirt plucked the badge from my hand and studied it. "He waited for us to bend over and lay ours down, knowin' O'Kelly's main focus would be on us. Then he pulled out his peacemaker; without a word, he just raised it up and shot O'Kelly."

"He what? He just shot him?"

"Yep. Mexican O'Kelly got hit in the left

shoulder, just above the heart. Must have knocked him back ten feet."

"Was he dead?"

"Nope, but he dropped his carbine and lost the will to fight, that's for sure. That's the way you have to do it, son. You got to squeeze off that trigger before anyone gets a chance to think it through. Coosie could do that. Still can, I reckon." Quirt rested his callused hand on my shoulder. "How much money do you have, Little Brother?"

I jammed my hand in my jeans and yanked out a dime, three nickels and four pennies. "Whatever happened to Mexican O'Kelly?"

"He went to jail for about a year for robbin' railroad payroll. When he got out, he bought a little ranch north of Mancos. We used to stop by and visit whenever we were in the area." He handed me the package. "This is a fine badge, son. I should know, I've worn lots of them in my day."

I held the badge up to my chest and tried to imagine what it would look like to wear it. I figured the drunk at the Day-Lyte Club would have backed away sooner, had I flashed one of these. "Did Coosie go visit Mexican O'Kelly, too?"

"Sure. In them days, you didn't take shootin' each other so personal. Most ever'one in the Southwest had ridden in a posse and been chased by a posse . . . sometimes in the same day." Quirt reached into his shirt pocket. "Hold out your hand."

He dropped a quarter into it.

CHAPTER 29

With a shiny, metal badge pinned over my heart, I led the men out of Woolworth's, and into the drizzling Albuquerque rain. The scattered clouds dumped their dregs before drifting east.

Thad Brewer held the door open for me. "That was nice of you to deputize Little Brother, Quirt."

Quirt slid across to the middle of the front seat. "I needed me some backup that wasn't readin' dime novels or stuck in the men's room."

"I said the door jammed. I didn't say I was stuck," Coosie insisted as he waited for Shorty and Thad to slip in next to me.

Bronc slammed his door. "One thing I don't miss about the old days is outhouses. The dadgum door was always sprung so it wouldn't close, or it was so stuck you had to kick it open. You'd freeze your, eh . . . tail off in the winter, and the smell in the summer could cripple the strongest of men."

Granddaddy honked his horn, then shot out into the Central Avenue traffic. I closed my eyes and gritted my teeth when I heard brakes squeal, but there was no crash or tinkle.

"Did you boys know Outhouse Dan?" Coosie called out.

"From Pueblo?" Bronc said.

125

"I think he was originally from Scottsbluff, Nebraska, but he might have spent time in Pueblo," Coosie replied.

"I never met him," Thad Brewer said, "but used his handiwork on more than one occasion."

"He built the best ones, that's for sure," Shorty added. "I reckon some are standin' to this day."

Granddaddy's blue eyes narrowed in the rear-view mirror. "He just built outhouses?" I asked.

He milked the accelerator in time with the slap of the windshield wipers. "That's it, son. Just outhouses. Nowadays we'd call it specialization." He pulled up at a stoplight behind a pale-green, '47 Studebaker. "Do you boys know how Dan got started?"

"Didn't he work for the U. P.?" Coosie offered.

"Yep, he was a tie cutter out of Virginia Dale, Colorado," Granddaddy said.

"What's a tie cutter?" I asked.

Coosie yanked an unwrapped peppermint out of his pocket and handed it over to me, then popped one into his own mouth. "In the early days, they cut all the railroad ties east of Utah by hand. Those boys were called tie cutters. They worked by the piece and got paid according to however many they got done in a day. Sometimes the men were in such a hurry to make more money, they cut 'em too short, or they had a flaw, or were too skinny. These rejects got tossed back."

"Used up for firewood, I heard," Shorty said.

Granddaddy honked his horn, but I couldn't see why. He glanced back at me. "The Union Pacific inspected the ties and paid for them at the siding just west of Laramie. The tie cutters would often set up a makeshift camp and wait to be paid. Some of them were a little embarrassed to use a sagebrush men's room, what with passenger trains rollin' through all the time, so ol' Dan up and built them a stout outhouse using those railroad tie rejects. People began to notice and put in orders for more."

"Did the U. P. give him them ties?" Shorty asked.

"At first they did, but then Dan said he bought them at two-cents each. He had to keep the tie yard tidy," Granddaddy explained. "So he went to building them stout outhouses of his."

"Built them on skids, didn't he?" Bronc added.

"Yep," Grandpa said. "He forked the skids together with a peg at the back so you could loop it with your reata and drag that sucker over the new hole. A man could move one of Outhouse Dan's without ever climbin' out of the saddle."

Coosie rubbed his fleshy jaws. "Not only that, the dadgum kids couldn't tip it over at Halloween."

"But even Outhouse Dan's buildin's weren't foolproof." Bronc rolled down his window and spit tobacco out into the sprinkling rain. "Seems

127

to me someone in this rig had a rather embar-
rasin' incident near Pagosa Springs."

"I don't want to talk about it." Shorty's jaw
clamped rigid.

"What happened?" I asked.

"I don't want to talk about it," Shorty reiterated.

"If we are goin' to school this boy in the cowboy tradition, we have to warn him about care-
less ropin'," Bronc hooted.

"You see, Little Brother," Quirt Payton offered,
"although Shorty is just a slight fella, he has a
big heart."

"A big heart for women," Thad cut in.

Bronc guffawed. "A big heart for big women."

Coosie drew a round circle in the breath fog on
his window. "And there was this schoolteacher at
Buenavista school, south of Pagosa Springs, who
was rather large."

"But very nice lookin'," Shorty corrected.

Quirt glanced back over his shoulder at me.
"Although it was only a one-room school, they
had bought one of Outhouse Dan's units and
established it out back by the cedar patch."

"I surmise it had been there a season or two,"
Coosie said, " 'cause to discipline the older boys,
she had them dig a new hole."

"In them days," Granddaddy clarified, "lots of
schoolteachers lived in a room at the back of the
school. Miss Amelia Ainsworth was one of them."

"Her name was Ainsleywert . . . not Ainsworth,"

128

Shorty interjected. "If you are going to tell the whole blamed story, you might as well get it right."

"So Shorty comes a courtin' on a Saturday afternoon," Thad said.

"Sunday afternoon," Shorty corrected.

Bronc waved his huge hands. "And he has a bouquet of poppies."

"Blue lupine," Shorty insisted.

Coosie drew another circle in the fogged up window. "And as he rode by the outhouse, he noticed the new hole dug about twenty feet downhill from the previous one."

"So, bein' the gentleman that he is . . ." Bronc grinned.

"He up and decides to skid it on over the new hole for Miss Amelia," Thad said.

"Shorty's a good roper," Coosie declared. "So it was no problem to loop the peg and dally the rope to the saddle horn."

"But it didn't skid easy," Granddaddy said.

"No sir. It was on a slight downhill. When he spurred his horse, that outhouse slid real quick," Quirt said.

Thad chuckled. "But Shorty's horse was a bit snuffy."

"Was that the buckskin stallion you got from Wieppe Willie?" Coosie asked.

Shorty shook his head. "No, I bought that one from Jessie James."

"You knew Jessie James?" I gasped.

"Not that Jessie James," Shorty insisted. "This one run a livery down in Magdalena."

"Anyway, when the screamin' started," Bronc continued, "Shorty's horse panicked."

"What screaming?" I asked.

"From inside the outhouse," Coosie said.

"Someone was in there?"

"Not just anyone," Thad Brewer revealed. "Miss Amelia Ainsworth . . ."

"Ainsleywert," Shorty corrected.

"The schoolteacher was making death threats against the one doin' the draggin'," Bronc said.

"And when Shorty tried to apologize, she stuck her shotgun out the door and blasted him," Coosie said.

"She didn't shoot me," Shorty whined. "She just aimed in my general direction."

"She put a hole in your hat," Quirt declared.

"Probably a ricochet."

"Why did she take a shotgun to the privy?" I questioned.

Shorty McGuire patted my knee. "Snakes, Little Brother. Some ladies don't like the possibility of snakes sleepin' in the outhouse."

"Whatever happened to that schoolteacher?" Thad inquired.

Shorty rubbed his wide mustache. "She moved to Shiprock and married the Indian agent. They

had six boys and two girls and retired in Prescott, Arizona."

"That could have been you, Shorty," Quirt remarked. "If only you had not tossed that loop."

Grandpa parked just off the alley behind the Matador Hotel and set the emergency brake.

Shorty piled out of the car after me. "Yeah, but then I would have missed sittin' around the lobby of the Matador, swappin' stories and swattin' flies."

We shuffled through the back doorway of the Matador.

I heard Shorty sigh. "Yeah, but you got to admit Prescott's nice this time of the year," he said, quiet-like.

CHAPTER 30

A boy of about seventeen stood at the registration counter of the Matador. He banged on a bell as if he played a time-limited pinball machine.

Quirt Payton eyed the front door as he headed over to the boy. The rest of us tagged along behind. "Anything we can do for you, son?"

"Doesn't anyone work here?"

"They must be detained elsewhere," Shorty offered.

"Can we help you out?" Coosie said.

"I'm supposed to deliver a note to Miss Diane Anderson."

"She's probably in the back room," Granddaddy explained. "Are you from Western Union?"

The boy surveyed the room as if expecting someone else to enter. "Do I look like a delivery boy? A guy in the side alley gave me two bucks if I give her this note. For two bucks, I don't have all day."

Quirt held out his hand. "I'll give it to her."

The boy hesitated. "But I get the whole two bucks."

"Yep," Quirt said.

The boy glanced over his shoulder. "Okay . . ." He shoved a folded piece of paper in Quirt's hand, spun on the heels of his high-top, black, tennis shoes and trotted out the front door.

"Now, there's a boy in a hurry," Bronc said.

Shorty pointed to the paper. "You goin' to open the note, Quirt?"

"It ain't for us to read." He tucked the folded note into his vest pocket. "I'll go scout out Miss Diane."

"You know your way back, don't ya?" Bronc prodded.

Quirt Payton didn't respond, but made sure his brown suit coat flipped open to show the walnut grips of his revolver.

"Speakin' of notes, did I ever tell you about the missing letter from that gal in Denver?" Bronc said. "If it weren't for that, I'd have probably married and settled down."

"Can't imagine you married," Shorty teased.

"I can," Granddaddy added.

"Did the mail lose your letter?" I asked.

"Nope."

"The mail lost a letter of mine," Coosie huffed. "And I will never forgive them for that."

"I had lots of mail that took a while to catch up with me. I suppose that happens to us all," Thad said. "I had one piece that had thirteen postmarks."

Coosie pulled his teeth out and rubbed his gums.

"What was the letter that the Post Office lost, Mr. Harte?" I asked.

He coughed deep before slipping his teeth back in. "It was a note from my Aunt Feora sayin' that my mama had died of pneumonia. It was in 1918 and she took the flu, then it got worse. I didn't get that letter until 1921. It was a sad day for me. Folks back home didn't think I even cared enough to come to Mama's funeral. I went home as soon as I got the word, but it was too late. My older brother wouldn't even speak to me."

"But that wasn't your fault."

"Not the way he sees it. My sisters all up and moved East, so I haven't heard from them in years. Aunt Feora still writes."

"You have an aunt still alive?"

Coosie laughed and slapped his hand on my shoulder. "Ain't that somethin'?"

Bronc leaned on the registration desk. "At least you have someone to blame. I have to bear it all myself."

"Did you lose a letter, too?" I asked.

"No, the letter was there, but I just didn't see it in time." Bronc gazed across the massive, empty lobby. "Her name was Miss Claudia."

I peered into the back room, but couldn't see Miss Diane or anyone. "Who's Miss Claudia?"

"The gal who wrote me the lost letter. She worked at the Front Range Café in Denver," Bronc said.

Shorty tugged at his mustache. "Was that the joint that ol' Sherb Wanamaker ran?"

"No, that was the Front Club in Colorado Springs," Thad corrected.

Shorty cleared his throat. "Didn't his brother . . ."

Coosie rubbed his smooth-shaven chin. "Nope, you're thinkin' of Herb Whittaker . . ."

"But I thought . . ."

"It was that Italian baker . . ." Granddaddy announced.

"Louisi?" Thad quizzed.

"No, Bianco," Bronc explained.

I tugged on Grandpa's shirt sleeve.

"Some stories, Little Brother, don't need to be told," he said.

I chewed on my lower lip. "I'd still like to hear about Bronc's lost letter."

Quirt Payton stomped out into the high-ceilinged lobby. "She ain't here, boys. Emily's foldin' towels, but she said she hasn't seen Miss Diane since noon."

"Didn't she make it back on the bus?" Thad said.

"I should have gone with her," Quirt fumed.

Bronc waved his massive arms. "She's a big girl and don't need our help to ride a bus."

Shorty pulled off his hat and scratched his thin, gray hair. "But where did she go?"

"Maybe she's in trouble," I said.

"I reckon she has her own schedule and don't

need us makin' decisions for her," Granddaddy cautioned.

"Maybe we ought to read that note," Shorty suggested.

"If a person wanted ever'one to read it, it wouldn't be folded," Quirt explained.

Thad Brewer rubbed on his thumbless hand. "What are we goin' to do?"

"I'll tell you this, boys, I'm ready to sit down," Coosie said. "Little Brother, do you want to play some cribbage?"

I pushed my straw hat back. "Yes, but I won't play you penny-a-point because I spent all my money on my new badge."

"The way Coosie's been playin' lately, you would have won yourself a fortune," Thad hooted.

The old cowboys followed my lead as we shuffled back across the huge, empty lobby.

"Them flowers are gone," Bronc exclaimed.

Shorty sauntered around the lobby table. "She must have come back and got them."

"Maybe Emily knows what happened to them," Quirt murmured, then shuffled back to the hotel office.

Bronc plopped down on the leather sofa. "This is funny, boys."

"I don't see nothin' that funny," Shorty mumbled.

Bronc shook his head. "Do you know how

excitin' our days are? We get all stirred up 'cause them dadgum flowers are missin'."

Thad blew his big nose on his bandanna. "Are you sayin' we live dull lives?"

"Dull, boring, routine," Coosie admitted. "I reckon you name it. What was the most excitin' thing that happened in the past year? Not you, Pop . . . or Little Brother . . . but those of us that live at the Matador."

"That's a toss-up," Thad whooped. "It was either when the water main busted on the second floor last January and we all had to move out of our rooms in the middle of the night . . . or it was when little Florence, the poodle, peed on Mrs. Roseberg's Christmas tree and she fainted dead away. She purtneer broke Shorty's ribs."

"I can still feel a twinge in my back. Why did I try to catch her?" Shorty muttered.

"I remember one time up on Black Mesa," Coosie rambled. "We'd been on fall gather for eight weeks. It was gettin' down to six or seven degrees ever' night, and wood for fires was scarce. My toes was numb all day, and if I put them by the fire, they hurt like a train ran over them. My gritty duckin's rubbed my legs like coarse sandpaper. The fingers of my gloves were worn clean through. We had to chase off a gang of rustlers out of Eagleton. We knew they was out there, just waitin' for another opportunity. So we didn't sleep well."

"Was that the time Black Nose Ross was so tired he fell out of the saddle and slept face down in the snow?" Bronc asked.

"Yep," Coosie said. "Ever' one of us was actin' touched in the head. Ol' Hub Bacon saddled up one mornin' buck naked. Said if he was goin' to freeze to death, he might as well go ahead and get it over with."

"That's ol' Hub for you. He was always in a hurry," Granddaddy said.

"And had fast horses," Shorty added.

"Did he freeze to death?" I asked.

Coosie tugged at his tight collar. "Nope. When a couple Kiowa women showed up sellin' firewood, he jerked on his clothes faster than Jack Sprat."

"Where's this story goin', Coosie?" Thad pressed.

"Just this." Coosie struggled to lean forward. "I remember me and Pokey Patterson sittin' there wonderin' if we'd ever be warm again. And I told him, 'Some day, Poke . . . I'll quit this cowboy business and live in a fine hotel with clean sheets, warm room, and tasty food.' "

"That's what we have now," Thad said.

Coosie sighed. "Well, it's usually hot, humid and I can't taste much of anything, but the sheets are clean."

Bronc stretched his legs out. "If you had the

138

strength, would you chuck it all and go out with the wagon again?"

"In a heartbeat," Coosie replied.

Quirt Payton stomped across the room. His bootheels slapping against the hardwood floor summoned our full attention. "Miss Emily found the vase of flowers busted in the middle of the lobby. She cleaned up the mess and tossed the flowers in a bucket in the back room."

CHAPTER 31

"It ain't like Miss Diane to make a mess like that, then walk off and leave it," Shorty said.

"How do we know what she'd do?" big Thad said. "Until a few hours ago, we hadn't spoken to her much."

"Except for Quirt. He seems to know his way around the back room," Bronc said.

"If you are accusin' me of somethin', you better make it clearer than that," Quirt Payton fumed.

Thad Brewer grinned. "What does that remind you of, Pop?"

Granddaddy patted my head then pulled his fixings out of his shirt pocket. He rolled another quirley. "The time the Rockfield twins said the same words to ol' Navel-Less."

Thad motioned to Granddaddy and he passed the tobacco fixings. "Navel told them that it would be healthier for ever'one if there were six mules in the corral when he finished eatin' his supper."

"Was he in the Navy?" I asked.

"No, Little Brother," Granddaddy explained. "Not n-a-v-a-l, but n-a-v-e-l. He didn't have a bellybutton, so he got the nickname, Navel-Less. Anyway, one of the twins . . . I couldn't never remember which was Albert and which was

Alfred . . . said, 'If you are accusin' us of some-thin', you'd better make it clearer than that.' "

"But a man has to have a bellybutton," I protested.

"Ol' Navel pulled out his revolver and laid it on the table to the right of his plate," Thad said. "Then he yanked out his boot gun and laid it to the left of his plate."

"Everyone has a bellybutton!" I complained louder.

"Adam and Eve didn't," Shorty offered.

Granddaddy ignored me and Shorty. "Waving a steak knife as big as ol' Jim Bowie's, Navel hollered loud enough for ever'one on both sides of the Rio Grande to hear."

"What do you mean, Adam and Eve didn't have bellybuttons?" I protested.

"As I recollect," Thad chimed in, "Navel called them horse thieves, drunkards, slackers, morally degenerate and an embarrassment to humanity and would be happy to be more specific if there was any part of it they didn't savvy."

Coosie leaned back on the brown, leather sofa and roared with laughter. "Ol' Navel was about the best there was at sizin' a man up and puttin' him in his place."

Shorty McGuire leaned toward Granddaddy and me. "Little Brother, a bellybutton is just a scar of where you used to be tethered to your mama before you were born. Adam and Eve got created direct by the Good Lord, so they didn't have no scar."

Grandpa lit his hand-rolled cigarette and took a slow puff. "The line that sticks in my mind was when Navel called them 'worthless dung in the corral of life.'"

Thad handed Granddaddy's fixin's back. "Ol' Navel-Less was beggin' for a fight, that's for sure."

I yanked off my straw, cowboy hat and rubbed my forehead, then glanced up at Shorty McGuire. "You mean, Navel-Less didn't have a mama?"

"I think Navel would have loved to have an excuse to 'clean the corral', if you catch my drift," Granddaddy observed.

"Of course he had a mama, Little Brother," Shorty reassured me.

Grandpa took another drag on his quirley. "One of the twins growled, 'Are we goin' to let him talk to us like that?'"

Shorty lowered his voice and aimed it right at me. "Navel got injured in the Spanish War. He took a bayonet in the belly."

"The other twin eyed Navel's two pistols layin' on the table, then remarked, 'Well, I reckon he was mostly right,'" Granddaddy closed his eyes and laughed as if he had just seen it happen. "'But he called us worthless dung!' the other twin shouted."

"Was Navel with Teddy down in Cuba?" Bronc asked.

"Nope. But if I counted up the number I met that claimed to be with Teddy at San Juan Hill, I reckon he had two million cowboys on his side."

"So one of them Rockfields went for his holster," Thad continued, "but Navel had that Colt of his pointed and cocked and aimed at his head before his hand ever got to his grips."

Granddaddy shook his head. "That twin stammered, 'He's right about one thing . . . I reckon we could use a bath; it's been a long winter.' "

Shorty looked me in the eyes. "Navel got his belly cut up bad, but he was a heavyset man in those days. When the army doc sewed him up, he didn't have a bellybutton left, just a long scar, and after a few years the scar mostly went away."

Granddaddy took up the story with vigor. "Navel was on his feet with both guns, one pointin' at each of the Rockfield twins. Pappy Dimwitty asked him not to bloody up the café, 'cause he had just scrubbed it up from the Ortiz ruckus the week before."

"Was that the Ortiz from down at Lordsburg?" Coosie quizzed.

Thad shook his head. "No, this was the one from Española."

"Navel told the twins to march out to the alley, 'cause he was goin' to shoot them and he was in a hurry to get back to his cherry pie," Granddaddy continued.

Bronc rubbed his lips. "Pappy Dimwitty made the best cherry pie in New Mexico."

"It was the bacon grease," Coosie blurted out.

Shorty locked his fingers and cracked his knuckles. "Bacon grease?"

"He told me he used bacon grease in his pie crust," Coosie said.

"What happened to the Rockfield twins?" I asked.

"One of them hollered, 'You ain't goin' to shoot us, jist 'cause we borrowed a couple of ol' mules, are you?' " Granddaddy said.

Thad interrupted. "Navel stepped right up and laid the barrel of the .45 against his forehead and growled, 'Don't worry, Pappy, I'll help you scrub the blood off the floor.' "

"Did he shoot them?" I pressed.

"Nope." Granddaddy took a long drag on the quirley. "He said, 'All I want, boys, is six mules in the corral when I finish my pie.' 'We cain't return mules if we are dead!' one of the twins hollered. Navel brought his gun down. 'Now, that's the most intelligent thing I ever heard either one of you say.' He holstered his guns and ate on his pie."

"Guess what he found in the corral when he went out there?" Thad quizzed.

"Six mules?" I said.

"Seven," Granddaddy corrected. "Either they can't count, or they was feelin' extra guilty."

Quirt jumped to his feet. "We can't sit here tellin' windy stories. Miss Diane might be needin' us."

Thad cleared his throat, then coughed. "Do you reckon readin' that note will help us know what's goin' on?"

"What about it, Pop?" Quirt asked. "You're the conscience of this group."

Granddaddy nodded.

The other four did the same.

Quirt Payton plucked the note from his vest pocket and unfolded it slow like a telegram from the war department.

"What's it say, Payton?" Bronc roared.

Quirt pushed his wire-framed glasses up on his nose. "Meet me at the Pit at 4:00 and bring my box."

"That's it?" Shorty scratched his thin, gray hair.

Quirt Payton turned the note over. "Yep. That's it."

CHAPTER 32

"What in tarnation is the Pit?" Coosie demanded.

Thad leaned over the chair and spit in the spittoon. "I never did like that Leon."

"How do we know the note's from Leon?" I asked.

Bronc rubbed his square jaw. "The kid said a man paid him to deliver it."

Shorty twirled his hat in his hand. "He didn't say which man."

Quirt pulled off his spectacles, and cleaned them on a white handkerchief. "Leon knows there are people lookin' for him . . . and I don't reckon he wants to see us, either. I figure it's Leon."

"You reckon that's where Miss Diane is?" Granddaddy said. "At the Pit?"

"She didn't get this note yet," Quirt said. "So why would she be there?"

"Let me read that," Bronc stated.

Quirt pulled it back. "You think I didn't read it right?"

"Sometimes a letter or word read wrong can make all the difference."

"We don't have time for that story," Quirt insisted.

Bronc turned to me. "Little Brother, always

146

read your letters careful. It could make all the difference in the world."

"I'm going to go ask Emily if she knows anything about the Pit," Quirt declared.

"I don't think it's rainin' out," Shorty said. "I'll go down to ol' Fugi's grocery and ask around. They know ever'thin' there is to know."

"I'll take a look at the phone book," Thad offered. "Maybe the Pit is a joint like the Day-Lyte Club."

Coosie scooted to his feet, "I'll go up and check with Mrs. Dabroski. She knows ever'thin' about ever'body in Albuquerque. But, if I don't return in ten minutes, you got to rescue me."

"If you ain't back in ten minutes, we'll come rescue Mrs. Dabroski," Bronc hooted.

"Katie's sister's girl works in the sheriff's office. I'll telephone her and see if she's heard of the Pit." Granddaddy sauntered toward the payphone booth at the back of the lobby.

I glanced up at Bronc. "Are you takin' off, too?"

He shook his head. "If them five can't find the Pit, I don't reckon I could add to it. Besides, I got a story to tell you."

"About the lost letter?"

"This is what happened. I met a gal in Denver when I was just a young buck, maybe twenty-four or -five. Her name was Miss Claudia St. Claire. I'll admit that I got carried away with her charms. When Bob Robertson asked me to run the winter line camp up on the Milk River, I invited Miss Claudia if she'd move up there with me."

"You asked her to marry you?"

"I reckon that's what I did."

"What did she say?" I pressed.

"I got run out of town before she answered."

"How come?"

"Hole-diggin' Rufugio Perez and me had partnered up, and he got into a fight with Crazy Penny. She came after Rufugio with two knives, a shotgun and ball-and-cap revolver."

"How did she carry all of that?" I asked.

Bronc shook his head. "You don't want to know, Little Brother. Anyway, we had to leave in a hurry, 'cause Crazy Penny was workin' for Harlan Biggers, and he was a mean son . . . eh . . . he was mean, son."

"So you never knew how Miss Claudia would have answered you?"

"Oh, I found out. That knowledge haunts me to this day."

"Did you see her again?"

"Never saw her another moment in my life. I was herdin' agency beef up to Deer Lodge, so when we hit the Northern Pacific track west of Billings there was a note from Miss Claudia."

"What did it say?"

"She said she would go with me to the Milk River."

"She'd marry you?"

"I reckon that's what she said. Anyway, the note said, 'I'll be in Tree Forks until the first of the month. If you don't show by then, I'll know your answer.' "

"Tree Forks?"

"Yeah, it was a tiny little stage stop on the trail up to Ft. Benton. I told the boys to push the cattle without me and took off on a trot to Tree Forks."

"Was she waitin' for you?"

"I had me a sorrel gelding that lamed up about White Sulfur Springs. I lost a couple of days until I, eh, Indian traded him for a spotted horse."

"Indian traded?"

"That's what we called it when you left your horse and took another. . . . without askin'."

"You stole a horse?"

"No, I just traded without askin'. I brought the horse back a week later."

"Was she waiting for you at Tree Forks?" I pressed.

Bronc let out a deep sigh. "Nope. I figured I had arrived there before she did. I mean, she didn't know when I'd actually be there. So, I just waited for her."

"How long did you wait?"

"Until the first of the month."

"She didn't show?"

"Nope."

"You think she changed her mind?"

"Hard to tell, Little Brother. I figured maybe she got there before me and got cold feet waitin' on me. So I rode south about as melancholy as a man can be. I kept readin' her note over and over. When the sun was goin' down that day, I held the letter up with the sunlight behind it. And there it was."

"What was?"

"The lost letter."

"There were two letters?"

"Not a letter letter but a letter of the alphabet."

"You mean like an $a - b - c$?" I questioned.

"I mean an h. It wasn't Tree Forks she went to, but Three Forks. Her pen needed more ink, and the h was faded out. I could see the indentation in the paper. She meant that I should meet her in Three Forks."

"Where's that?"

"Between Bozeman and Butte . . . no more than a day's ride from where the herd was in the first place."

"Did you go there?"

"Yep." Bronc stared at the top of his boots.

"Was she still there?"

"Nope. Friends said a yellow-haired lady stayed a week at the hotel, then left on the train west."

"And you never saw her again?"

"Nope."

"But . . . you could have been married, had a family and owned a big ranch in Montana."

"And not slept on hard ground or in cheap hotels all my life. Yeah, I think about that most ever' mornin'. Always read your letters careful, Little Brother."

"Yes, sir, I will."

Grandpa meandered back across the lobby from the payphone about the same time Quirt Payton emerged from the hotel office.

"Did you have any luck, Pop?" Bronc called out.

Grandpa rubbed his bony, arthritic knuckles. "Yep, it helps to have kin in the right place."

"You found out where the Pit is?" Quirt quizzed.

"Sure did." Grandpa patted my shoulder.

"So did I," Quirt beamed.

The big front door banged open. "Hey, boys," Shorty called out, "wait until you hear what the Pit is."

CHAPTER 33

Thad Brewer's worn, brown boots scuffed across the polished, wooden floor of the hotel lobby, as he waved a telephone book. "I think I found it, boys."

"Well, that makes four of us," Quirt said. "Where's the old man?"

"Coosie went up to see widow Dabroski," Bronc explained. "You reckon someone ought go fetch him?"

Quirt Payton glanced around. "Other than Pop, if any of you was visitin' a widow lady, would you want us to come beatin' on the door?"

"If it was Mrs. Dabroski, I surely would," Thad Brewer mumbled.

"Coosie said for us to come rescue him," Bronc reported.

"You want to go get him?" Thad challenged.

"Eh, no," Bronc admitted.

Shorty waved his hands. "Remember that time down in Nogales, Arizony . . ."

"It was Douglas," Coosie corrected.

"When Tell-It-All Thompson . . ."

"Tell-It-All Thomas," Thad interrupted.

"Was lookin' for Joe White . . ."

Granddaddy cleared his throat. "Jim White."

" 'Cause they had stolen them horses . . ."

"Cows," Quirt explained.

Shorty's face flushed red. "From the Double Bar G ranch . . ."

"Double 0 G," Granddaddy said.

"In Patagonia . . ."

Thad shook his head. "Ft. Huachuca."

"And the Arizona Rangers was . . ."

"U.S. marshals," Quirt explained. "I ought to know."

"The marshals was after them and Tell-It-All had the horses in the alley. They wasn't five blocks from the Mexican border, but when he banged open Joe White's door . . ."

"Jim White," I corrected.

"Ol' White reached for his holster that was hanging on the chair . . ."

"The bedpost," Thad grinned.

"And growled, 'Don't ever barge in on a man who's visitin' a lady.' "

"Actually," Bronc interjected, "he said, 'visitin' a . . .' "

Granddaddy cleared his throat real loud.

Bronc's brown eyes flashed over at me. "Yep . . . Shorty's right . . . he said, 'visitin' a lady.' "

"Then old Joe . . ."

"Jim," we all corrected.

"Shot Tell-It-All in the leg."

"He shot the lintel above the door," Quirt declared.

"And pitched such a fit that the Rangers . . ."

"Marshals," I stated.

"Caught up with them before they made it to Mexico. Yep, as long as I live, I'll never forget that," Shorty boasted, then turned to me. "Don't be in a hurry to bust into the room of a compadre when he's visitin' a lady. If you got to do it, Little Brother, always have your pistol drawn."

Quirt nodded at the little man with the big mustache. "Shorty, you want to go get Coosie, then we'll sort out what we found out?"

"Let Little Brother go. He's got young legs to climb them stairs."

"Is that okay with you, Pop?" Quirt asked.

"Sure, what room is the widow Dabroski in?"

"Two-twenty-two," Quirt Payton reported.

I repeated the number back to him.

"Ol' Quirt has ever' room memorized. He can usually tell you the name of the one-nighters, too," Coosie said.

"What do I tell him?" I asked.

"Tell him we need to saddle up and ride," Shorty hooted. "Why, the Pit is on the other side of town."

"That ain't what I heard," Quirt corrected.

"Go get Coosie," Granddaddy urged me.

"But you can't talk about the Pit until I get back. You promise?" I whined.

Quirt Payton held up his right hand. "Scout's honor, Little Brother."

Looking back, I'd have to say the Matador

Hotel stunk of old sweat and dirt and fifty years of hard living. But at the time, when I mentioned the odor, Grandpa just called it the "smell of history." To Granddaddy, and the old cowboys, history reigned as king. He once told me that only the Lord above knew more about us than history. History ruled New Mexico long before Juan de Onate set up shop just north of Española. And history would continue to exist after all of us was gone.

For Granddaddy and his cowboy pals, history was real. You could see it in the cowboys' eyes. You could hear it in their stories. You could touch it when you brushed against their Colts or Winchesters or chaps or Stetsons. You could taste history's fine dust ever' time a dirtdevil swirled off the hills and down Central Avenue. And on that day in 1954, I could smell history in the second story hallway of the Matador Hotel.

Either that, or it was just sweat, dirt and fifty years of hard life.

I parked outside of Room 222 and took a deep breath. I tugged down my straw hat, pulled out a cap pistol and tapped on the door.

I got no response.

I grabbed the barrel of the gun and was about to tap on the door with the grip, when it swung open.

In front of me stood a very wide woman, with gray-blue hair. A red ring on her finger flashed brighter than them you get in a Cracker-Jack box. "Young man, it will work better if you hold the other end of that gun."

I blushed and holstered my gun. "Yes, ma'am."

"Now, is this a stickup or are you selling 'Grit' magazine subscriptions?"

I yanked off my hat and rocked back on my heels. "No, ma'am. I've got a message for Mr. Harte. Is he here?"

"Son, it isn't polite to ask a lady if she has a man in her room."

"Eh . . . well . . . I didn't . . . I mean . . . excuse me, ma'am." I tipped my straw hat.

"If I happen to see Mr. Harte, what would you like me to tell him?"

"Tell him it's time to saddle up and ride."

"What?"

"Me and the boys are waitin' for him in the lobby."

She had thick, red lipstick and crooked teeth but a very pleasant laugh. "You know, son . . . no matter how old they are . . . cowboys are boys, aren't they? So you and the boys need Mr. Harte to ride in your posse?"

"Yes, ma'am, if you can spare him," I stammered. "I mean, if he was here and you could spare him."

"You're learning, son." She turned and called out. "Horace, I believe you are wanted downstairs."

Coosie grabbed his hat and hurried out the door. Halfway down the hall, he stopped me and bent low. I smelled peppermint. "Little Brother, if you ever tell a livin' soul that my name is Horace, I will put the curse of Guadalupe Baca on your children and your children's children."

I sucked in a deep breath, then blurted out, "I won't tell anyone ever!"

"I know you won't." Coosie shoved a couple peppermints into my hand. "Besides, you came just in time. I don't think I could sit through another yarn."

"She was telling stories?"

"No," Coosie grumbled. "She was loopin' yarn and usin' my hands as a spool."

"Did you find out about the Pit?"

The old man shuffled along. "Yes, I did, Little Brother. And it ain't as complicated as you might surmise."

CHAPTER 34

"Ol'-timer, we're mighty glad you are still mobile!" Bronc saluted as me and Coosie hiked over to the worn, brown leather chairs and divan.

Coosie put his arm on my shoulder as we parked in front of the flowerless lobby table. "The boy pulled me out of a tight one, that's for sure. Reminds me of the time Pop rescued me from that snake den down in the Blue Mountains. Remember that, Pop?"

Grandpa tugged at the buttoned collar of his white shirt. Tradition kept it fastened, no matter how warm the room. "Oh, I remember it. I'm amazed that you do."

"Was ol' Coosie soused?" Thad asked.

"Nope," Coosie rubbed his round, fleshy chin. "That was the first time I realized I had diabetes, boys. I had stopped in at Gretchen's in Bisbee and ate me an entire pecan pie. Too much sugar, they tell me now. At the time I figured Gretchen was just tryin' to get even for that prank with dead chickens."

"I was in on that prank," Shorty blurted out. "I don't remember you being with us, Coosie."

"I wasn't. I was takin' Charlie Bride's body back to Tucson before it turned sour."

"That's right, now I remember," Shorty nodded.

"But Gretchen thought I was in on it," Coosie continued. "I surmised at the time that she poured the pie with cod liver oil or somethin' as vile."

"I heard you never made it to Tucson," Quirt remarked.

"Nope. It was July-hot, and by the time I got to the tracks at Benson, the body smelled so bad they wouldn't let me load it up on the train. Not even the empty flatcar," Coosie explained.

"What did you do?" I asked.

"I buried him in Benson, and telegraphed his kin in Tucson to tell them they could come dig him up and move him whenever they wanted," Coosie said.

"You reckon they ever done it?" Thad posed.

"No. The strange thing is, the telegraph came back sayin' that Charlie didn't have any kin in Tucson."

"But Charlie went to visit his mother in Tucson ever' Christmas," Shorty said.

"Come to find out, he just stayed at a boarding house," Coosie said. "He didn't have any family to his name, but he didn't want anyone to know."

The room grew silent.

Coosie let out a long, slow sigh. "Pop, you are a lucky man. Everybody needs some family."

"I got me a tribe of nieces and nephews back in Oklahoma," Thad said. " 'Course I don't even know their names."

159

When the room got silent again, I exclaimed: "Did you really fall in a snake hole, Mr. Harte?"

"Not a snake hole," Coosie explained. "A snake pit. Must have been a dozen of them down there. Snakes is that way. Sort of clannish, I reckon. But your Granddaddy was a strong man. He pulled me out of there by the shirt collar, without a single snake bite. Don't make partners like Pop anymore."

Bronc bellowed, "They don't make shirts like that anymore!"

"Is the snake pit still there?" I asked. "I've never seen a snake pit."

"There's plenty of snake pits still up in them mountains," Coosie declared. "But I cleaned that one out the next spring."

I leaned forward and tugged on my ear. "How did you do that?"

"Why, I tossed a pig in there," Coosie said.

"You did what?" I puffed.

Coosie plopped down on the big, brown divan. "I bought me a pig from them farmers down at the flats. What was their name?"

"Was that the ones with that big girl named Norma?" Shorty asked.

"Nope, they was down the road. This was that little unpainted cabin in the cottonwoods," Coosie said.

"Largemouth?" Thad quizzed.

"Yeah, that was them. Well, I stopped by and . . ."

"They all had large mouths?" I asked.

"No, Little Brother, their name was Large-mouth." Coosie's eyes flashed impatience. "Anyway I bought me a two-dollar pig. Carried him across the cantle like a sick calf all the way up to that snake den. I tied a rope halter around him and tossed him down there. I told him as soon as he was done with breakfast, I'd pull him up and turn him loose to run free in the Blues."

"Was that where them wild pigs came from?" Shorty inquired.

Coosie flashed a toothless grin. "Yep, I reckon he partnered up with a javelina sow."

"Pigs eat snakes?" I grimaced.

"Yep," Bronc replied. "They eat 'em just like you and me eat strawberries. I reckon they taste like dessert to a pig."

I swallowed hard. "But . . . but . . . don't the snakes bite him?"

Coosie rubbed his hand across his bald head. "Sure they do. But pigs got so much fat on 'em, that the poison never reaches the bloodstream. He had 'em cleaned out by evenin', so I turned him loose. A man has to keep his word, even if it is a pig."

"Why talk pigs?" Bronc growled. "What are we goin' to do about Miss Diane?"

"I figure it's time to load back up in Pop's Plymouth," Quirt said. "Miss Emily said the Pit is a nickname for Pittswalker's Café down by the river. She said for years ever'one just called it the Pit."

"We've been in this hotel since before the war, some of us longer, and we never heard of Pittswalker's," Coosie said.

"That's where Maddie Nation used to work, but it was called something else back then," Thad stated.

"It was called Angel's, wasn't it?" Shorty said.

"That place?" Coosie slapped his knee as if tryin' to keep it from fallin' asleep. "I thought it burned down years ago."

"You're thinkin' of Angelita's," Granddaddy said.

"Maybe so," Coosie said.

"Don't matter, 'cause that ain't the real Pit," Thad announced. "The answer is right here in the phone book."

CHAPTER 35

The way Thad Brewer's big hand dwarfed the Albuquerque phone book, I had no doubt he could rip it in two. Or anything else for that matter. He opened to the yellow pages.

"There it is," he pointed. "The Pit. It's an automobile supply and garage. They specialize in custom and racing cars. We all know Leon works at the Standard Station and likes fancy cars."

Shorty McGuire scooted up to the front of the chair. "Speakin' of fancy cars, remember the time the boys from the Rockin' Double J was comin' home from town in that ol' Model T of Pencil Lead Pete's? How does that story go?"

Thad Brewer cleared his throat. "There was six of 'em piled in it as I recall."

"Seven," Bronc interrupted.

"I heard it was six," Thad said.

"I should know, I was one of the seven," Bronc admitted.

Coosie rubbed his bald head. "You were?"

"That's what they tell me." Bronc glanced over at me. "I was asleep during the whole thing, Little Brother."

"Maybe you ought to tell it. If you was there," Thad suggested.

"You all go ahead. You probably remember it

better than me," Bronc mumbled.

"The way I hear it the boys of the Rockin' Double J had been to town to celebrate the fall gather." Thad scratched his thumbless hand. "When was that, Bronc? About 1930?"

"Must have been after ol' FDR took office." Bronc peered into an empty coffee cup. "It wasn't durin' Prohibition, that's for sure."

"Anyway," Thad continued, "I hear the boys decided to race a railroad train from Clement's Siding to the barranca at Arroyo Verde."

"Race a whole train?" I quizzed.

Thad shrugged. "I reckon it seemed like a good thing at the time."

"Back in them days, Little Brother," Granddaddy explained, "dirt roads ran alongside ever' train track. Sometimes it was the regular highway, and sometimes just a little more than a trail the train crew and telegraph men used. They were rough roads in places. Most had been cut with a mule-drawn, Fresno scraper."

"Say, did I ever tell you about that Armenian lady from Fresno who wanted me to dance at her wedding?"

"Shorty, let Thad finish. Besides, the last time you told that one, it was a Greek lady," Quirt said.

Shorty rubbed his mustache. "I get 'em confused."

"So," Thad continued, "them boys from the

Rockin' Double J honked their horn at the locomotive, and the engineer honked back and revved the old gal until them rails was whistlin'. Wasn't it about seven miles to the arroyo?"

"That's what I'm told," Bronc nodded. "I know for a fact it was a rough seven miles."

"How do you know that? You were asleep," I blurted out.

"Wait for the rest of the story, Little Brother," Granddaddy cautioned.

"So they was hoopin' and hollerin' and firin' pistols in the air and havin' a good race . . ." Thad said.

I chewed on my tongue and avoided lookin' at Grandaddy. "Didn't that noise wake you up, Mr. Bronc?"

Bronc winked at me. "I reckon I was quite sleepy."

"As I heard it," Thad said, "the boys won the race, so to speak. Beat the train by a couple hundred yards."

I tugged on my lower lip. "What do you mean, so to speak?"

"Oh, they won, alright, but just as they reached the edge of the arroyo, they remembered they didn't have any way to stop that Model T. Brakes in them days didn't stop quick and they was too close to the edge."

My hand covered my lip. "What happened?"

"They flew off the edge of the arroyo into air

165

and landed fifty feet below on top of some scrubby mesquite trees. Not a one of them six had a broken bone. Just bumps and bruises." Thad shook his head. "The Lord smiled on 'em that day."

"You mean, not one of the seven was hurt," I pressed. "Bronc was there, too."

"No, I wasn't," he murmured.

I felt my stomach drop. "But you said you were."

"No, I said I was in the car, not the canyon. Like I said, I was asleep. And the road kept dippin' down and back up." Bronc leaned back on the divan. "I woke up one time with an ache in my belly and stood up and mumbled, 'I need me some fresh air.' Right then we hit another of those bumps, swerved around the corner and I tumbled out."

"You fell out of the car?" I gasped. "Did you get hurt?"

"I reckon a few scratches and some bruised ribs when I hit them boulders," Bronc admitted. "I've been hurt worse, that's for sure."

"So you weren't in the Model T when it went over the edge?" I pressed.

"Nope."

"Then I was right," Thad said. "There was only six in that car."

"Six when it went over the edge," Bronc said. "I woke up the next mornin' with a ringin' headache and dragged back into town. That's

166

when I learned about the race that I missed."

"You surmise that Model T's still in the top of them mesquites?" Shorty pondered.

"I love to race horses, but not automobiles. They are as unpredictable as a Mexican revolution. You can't tell which way they will turn," Coosie said.

"Leon likes fast cars," Thad reiterated. "I'm sure this automobile parts store is the place."

Shorty McGuire paced the room. "I ain't too sure of that. Mrs. Fugiama down at the market claims the most famous place in Albuquerque that's called the Pit is that fancy Italian Restaurant just north of Del Oso Park. She said she sells an L.A. lug of yellow, crook-necked squash and a crate of bell peppers to them ever' Thursday."

"That's a lot of squash. A lug of okry would be nicer," Coosie mused.

"That ain't the Pit," Granddaddy declared.

"How do you know that?" Shorty quizzed.

"I took Katie to the Italian place on her birthday last July 6th. It's a fancy place, boys, with colored-glass chandeliers, white-linen tablecloths, and hand-painted pottery plates. They have enough silverware around ever' plate to make a nice weddin' gift for triplets."

"What's your point, Pop?" Quirt asked.

"Can you imagine the likes of Leon going to a nobby place like that?"

"Nope. Pop's right," Quirt agreed. "Miss Diane might go there, but not ol' Leon. The Day-Lyte Club is his idea of fancy dinin'.'"

"I do have an answer." Granddaddy tapped his quirley out in the ashtray. "Elaine's daughter, Barbara, who works at the sheriff's office told me the Pit is the old gravel pit across the Rio Grande at Five Points."

"They ain't worked that in years," Bronc said.

"Nope. Barbara said it's a local hangout for the beer drinking, knife totin', drag racin' crowd. The sheriff's office gets a lot of calls of complaints about it," Granddaddy said.

"That's the kind of place I'd expect Leon to hang out. Wouldn't surprise me none if he had a cheap Japanese knife in his boot," Shorty said.

Bronc patted his boot. "This one ain't Japanese."

"Yeah, I can see Leon showin' up at a gravel pit, but I can't imagine Miss Diane ever doin' it," Quirt said. "That don't make sense."

"That's 'cause you got it all wrong, boys," Coosie stated. "The widow Dabroski told me the Pit is the that seldom-used loading dock at the old warehouse behind the hotel."

"That ain't much of a pit," Shorty complained.

"But she's spied some of the staff of the hotel head there for a little privacy. When you are down in the well of that loading dock, she said, no one can see you. Not even from the hotel."

"I wonder why Emily didn't tell me that?" Quirt asked.

"Maybe she didn't want to give away a staff secret," Bronc suggested.

"Sounds too simple to me," Thad answered. "I say it's that auto parts store."

"I agree it's too simple," Granddaddy said. "That's why I'll stick with the gravel pit."

"I've never been to a fancy eye-talian restaurant. I wouldn't mind packin' down a five-dollar meal once in my life," Shorty remarked.

"You been to Del Monico's in Prescott, haven't you?" Coosie challenged.

Shorty pushed his hat back. "Is that Italian?"

"It ain't Chinese," Thad replied.

Shorty licked his lips. "I like Chinese food as long as they don't serve me tea in them funny little cups."

"I reckon we could jist drive by each place to see what we could see. We can't just sit around tellin' lies. Maybe we'll figure it out as we drive around town." Quirt jammed on his hat, just as the front door of the Matador swung open. A blonde lady with a raincoat stomped in, carrying a small box.

"Or," I grinned, "we can just ask Miss Diane!"

CHAPTER 36

I trotted across the lobby towards the blonde lady with the charcoal-gray hat.

Her hand on my shoulder, she led me back across the lobby. She carried a cigar box in her other hand. "You boys still worried about me?"

"Emily told us them flowers got all busted and it set us to ponderin'," Quirt explained.

"Did she clean them up? Bless her heart. When I got back here, I was so mad at him about chasin' after that skinny dancer with a cheap permanent and dime-store shoes that I flung the vase on the floor. Do you know how it feels to get rejected for the looks of her?" she fumed.

"To tell you the truth, Miss Diane, we didn't see her," Quirt said.

"But it don't matter," Shorty declared. "Even if she looked like Betty Grable or Grace Kelly or that Marilyn Monroe, we wouldn't like her."

"If she looked like Miss Marilyn, we might like her a tad," Bronc replied.

"I ain't been taken by a picture-show star since Miss Clara Bow," Coosie commented.

"Where did you go, Miss Diane?" Quirt asked.

"I remembered that good old Leon had given me a cigar box of jewelry to keep for him," she explained. "I went home to retrieve it."

"Keep for him?" Quirt asked.

"He said it belonged to his mother. His trailer has been broken into, so he thought it would be safer at my place."

"He lives in a trailer?" Granddaddy asked.

"One of those Little Burro camping trailers that's parked over on that vacant lot behind the Standard Station," she reported.

"Where he works?" Shorty quizzed.

"Where he used to work."

Quirt pulled off his glasses and rubbed his nose. "He got fired?"

"I stopped by just now to give him back this junk. They said he drew his pay about an hour ago and told them he was quitting."

"Maybe them other boys is moving in close," Coosie offered.

"I had to quit a job in a hurry once," Shorty said. "I was workin' at the Rafter-T-Bench in Victoria Basin. Woke up one Sunday afternoon in the bunkhouse and there was a woman the size of the Alamo pounding on the door with a long-handled pair of horseshoe nippers. She was cursin' ever'one from my mother to my grandchildren."

"Do you have grandchildren?" I asked.

"No, but if I did, they would be cursed. I didn't remember who she was and was in no mood to find out, my head poundin' like it did. I had got in kind of late and left old Petey rigged up. I jumped in the saddle and tore off around the big house with her chasin' me on foot. She shouted words seldom heard outside of a prison. The old man came out to the porch and hollered at me what was wrong. I told him it looked like I needed to quit. He shouted to circle one more time if I could, and he'd toss me my pay."

"He wrote you out a check?" I asked.

"Pay was in silver and gold coins in them days, Little Brother," Shorty explained. "So I galloped by again and he tossed me a poke with my pay. I surely appreciated that. Then I galloped out of there and didn't slow down until I reached Rio Largo."

"Why was she chasin' you?" I asked.

"I ain't sure," Shorty rubbed his chin. "I think it had somethin' to do with a one-hundred-pound sack of flour and a wedding dress, but it's all a little fuzzy in my mind."

"I didn't ever quit a job, unless it was done," Quirt stated.

"No sir, Quirt, you're right about that. A man don't quit unless the work is done," Coosie added.

"Well, Leon quit. Where did he go?" Bronc inserted.

"The guys at the service station said he mentioned going to Tulsa," Miss Diane replied.

"I figure he went to California," Quirt said.

"What makes you say that?" I asked.

"If you had two hoodlums you didn't want to follow you, what direction would you head?" Quirt explained.

"The opposite direction than they think," Shorty said.

"You sayin' he jist told them he was headed for Tulsa, in case those two came snooping around?" I pressed.

Quirt nodded. "He was serious enough to quit his job and move off. They got something on him, that's for sure."

"He was quite fond of his California boots and hat," Coosie said.

Bronc folded his arms across his massive chest. "I wonder what they had on Leon?"

"He hasn't left town yet," I blurted out. "He wants Miss Diane to meet him at the Pit at 4:00 p.m."

She pivoted on those high-heels like a windmill in a tornado. "How do you know that, Little Brother?"

My chin dropped.

Quirt Payton came to my rescue. "About the time we got back to the Matador, a delivery boy brought you a message."

"Just a kid who said Leon gave him two dollars to deliver it," Shorty said.

Coosie rubbed his fingertips over his fleshy lips. "He was in a hurry to leave so we said we'd see that you got it."

"But we couldn't find hide nor hair of you and was plumb worried," Thad admitted.

"So, we took a gander at the note to try and figure out what was goin' on," Bronc said.

"But we're stymied." Quirt handed her the note.

Miss Diane Anderson studied the note, then grinned.

"Something funny, Miss Diane?" I asked.

"I'm just happy I'll get to see him one more time and tell him what a worthless jerk he is."

"Is that the possibles he's wantin' you to bring?" Coosie asked.

Miss Diane glanced at the cigar box. "The what?"

"The goods in the box," Coosie explained. "Is that what he wants?"

She waved it in front of us. "Yes, ironic, isn't it?"

"What's in the box, Miss Diane?" I asked.

Grandpa pinched my arm 'til it hurt. "You'll have to excuse the lad," he said. "He's learnin' quick, but still needs schoolin'." He turned to me. "Little Brother, never ask about a person's private belongin's."

Shorty McGuire hooted. "Remember that time Joe Bill asked that ol' trapper what he had in the doctor's satchel?"

"Joe Bill knew better," Bronc said. "It served him right."

"What did the trapper do?" I asked.

"Told Joe Bill that he had rattlesnakes in the bag," Shorty explained.

"But Joe Bill was feelin' touchy. He pulled his gun and said, 'I don't believe you. I think you got whiskey in there and won't share,' " Bronc said.

Shorty took up the account. "So the trapper said, 'Why don't you jist stick your hand in there and find out.' "

Thad gruffed, "Joe Bill was never one to back down from a taunt."

"I seen him jump a horse over the Poco Bueno ditch when it was runnin' full to the top on a dare," Granddaddy said.

"I heard about that," Coosie chimed in. "Lost a good horse, didn't he?"

"But what about the trapper's bag?" I insisted.

"Joe Bill stuck his hand in . . . let out with a holler . . . and jerked it back with a four-foot rattler still fanged to his hand," Shorty hooted. "We rolled on the floor and busted our sides laughin'."

I rubbed my arm. "But what happened to Joe Bill?"

"He nearly died," Shorty shrugged. "But I reckon he learned his lesson."

"He left his reckless ways soon after that. He raised a remuda of kids with his Mexican wife and ended up being the mayor of Escabosa," Quirt reported.

"Ain't it funny which ones survive? I surmised that Joe Bill would never see twenty-five," Coosie pondered. "I reckon the Lord has different plans than we can see."

I pulled off my straw cowboy hat. "Miss Diane, I'm sorry for askin' what's in the cigar box."

"Little Brother, you learn the Code from these old men, because the day will come there won't be anyone to teach it but you." She opened the top of the White Owl cigar box and flashed its contents to us.

"Jewels?" I choked. "It's full of fancy jewelry?"

"Cheap jewelry," she said. "Most of them I recognize from Woolworth's."

I rubbed my shiny U.S. Deputy Marshal's badge.

CHAPTER 37

Miss Diane passed the box around. "Isn't this a hoot? I'm holding a cigar box of junk jewelry for a two-timin', pea-headed, flat-tire changer."

"We do like your spunk, Miss Diane," Thad said.

Quirt studied the contents then passed it along. "Why do you figure he was worried about losin' this?"

"He said it belonged to his mother," she reported.

Coosie immediately closed the box and handed it back to Miss Diane. "That's reason enough to save it."

Bronc shook his head and sighed. "Wish I had somethin' that belonged to my mama. She was a fine woman. She took the flu and died way too young. I walked out of the house that day, saddled my gray gelding, and rode all the way to Brownsville. Took me three weeks. I never went back. My brother and sister buried her next to Daddy. I'll return some day and put flowers on her grave. I'm just not ready for it, yet."

"When did she die?" I asked.

"In Ought-Four, son." Bronc rubbed on the palms of his hands like he was Lady Macbeth. "Yeah, I wish I had somethin' of my mother's."

Coosie reached into his worn, brown, suit coat pocket. I expected him to pull out a peppermint. Instead, he laid down an off-white pearl button about the size of a dime. "That was on the dress they buried mother in. I didn't get back to the service, but Aunt Daisy, bless her heart, took a button off and mailed it to me. I've carried it ever' day since."

Thad pointed at the cigar box. "If those belonged to his mama, my opinion of Leon just raised a notch."

"Don't let it raise too high, boys," Miss Diane cautioned. "I tell you, that is modern jewelry that you can buy at Woolworth's right now, cheap silver plate and cut glass. I wonder if he thought I wouldn't know the difference."

Quirt's hand stroked his clean-shaven chin. "If this ain't his mother's, then it's a mystery, boys. If a man wants to leave town in a hurry, he won't stick around for a box of dime-store jewelry."

"Maybe there is a secret compartment in the cigar box," I suggested.

"Secret compartment?" Shorty repeated.

"Me and Grandpa listened to Sergeant Preston of the Yukon on the radio one time and Tundra Thompson tried to smuggle the map to the Lost Gulch mine out of town in a secret compartment in his lunch bucket. But the sergeant's dog, King, sniffed it out."

"I wish I had me a gold-mine map sniffin' dog," Bronc said.

"We had a dog at the bunkhouse on the Triple A who could sniff out tobaccy," Thad declared. "You'd just say, 'Poncho, go get my fixin's' and he'd come trottin' back in a minute with a tobaccy bag. 'Course, you never knew whose tobaccy he would fetch, a fact that caused more than one bunkhouse brawl."

"Brutus Gooseman owned a blind bulldog that could sniff out fig cookies," Shorty said. "But I never did like them cookies much."

Miss Diane dumped the contents of the box on the round, glass-covered table, then handed it to me. "What do you think, Little Brother, is there a secret compartment?"

I opened the lid and studied the small box. "I don't know. I ain't never seen a secret compartment before." I handed the empty box to Granddaddy.

While the others examined the box, I inspected the rings, pins and necklaces piled on the table. The bright-colored stones fascinated me. I picked up a silver ring with a big, red stone. "How can you tell this is just glass and not a real gem?"

Thad plucked it out of my hand. He raked the red stone across the glass tabletop. "If it don't cut glass . . . won't even scratch it, it ain't real."

I plucked up some of the other pieces of jewelry

and dragged them across the glass tabletop. The only mark they made was a trail in the dust.

"I reckon I could have been wrong." Quirt handed the jewelry box back to Miss Diane. "Maybe it's just sentimental junk. There surely isn't a secret compartment in this box."

"Knowing Leon, he might have thought there were precious jewels here," Granddaddy declared.

"Pop is right. His choice of women demonstrates he don't know a precious jewel when he sees one," Coosie noted.

Miss Diane's grin revealed straight, white teeth. "Boys, boys, boys. This would have been a horrible day had it not been for you."

"To tell you the truth, Miss Diane, you put a little zip in this day for us," Thad said.

I placed the ring in the box. "So what are you going to do now, Miss Diane?"

"Wait until 4:00 p.m., then go over to the Pit and give Leon a piece of my mind, as well as his precious treasure."

"By the way, just which Pit is it?" Quirt asked.

"Which Pit?"

"In the note, it said meet you at the Pit," Granddaddy said. "Is that the old gravel pit near Five Points?"

"I say it's that nobby Italian restaurant up north by the park," Shorty said.

She drug her fingertips across her red, faded

lipstick. "No, it's just that recessed loading dock at the empty warehouse across the alley."

"I told ya!" Coosie laughed. "And you derided me for goin' to visit the widow."

"Well, I'll swan . . ." Shorty said. "And I was all set for an Italian supper."

"The Round-Up Café has good spaghetti on Thursday nights," Bronc replied. "That's about as close to Italian as we get."

I scooped up all the jewels and dumped them back into the box. "What are you goin' to do now, Miss Diane?"

"I need to get some work done, so I don't lose my job. Meanwhile, I'll think of some choice words to call Leon."

"If you need some help findin' the right word," Bronc offered. "Between us, we probably know more words than an aircraft carrier full of sailors."

"Miss Diane," I blurted out. "I might say this wrong, but if you need some help, I could come with you. I ain't afraid of Leon."

"Well spoken, Little Brother," Coosie replied. "I reckon we'd all be obliged to come along."

"Help? No, I don't . . ." When she paused the most beautiful blue eyes in the world lit up. "Yes. That would be nice, Little Brother. I wouldn't mind having an audience. You are all invited to come with me to the Pit at four."

She strutted to the office.

"But what about Leon's jewelry?" I called out.

"I'm puttin' you in charge of watchin' them until four o'clock. You take good care of them."

Looking back fifty years later, I can still feel how Miss Diane's smile caused a lump in my throat.

CHAPTER 38

"What time is it, Coosie?" Shorty asked.

The old cowboy pulled his gold-plated pocket watch from his vest. "It's 2:24 and I'm hungry. I ain't had nothin' since breakfast but a glass of iced tea and a raspberry tart."

"You had a what?" Bronc choked.

"That widow is mighty friendly, ain't she?" Thad prodded.

"What do you mean by that?" Coosie snapped.

Thad Brewer shrugged. "I don't mean nothin', old man."

Coosie's hand slipped to his holstered revolver. "I ain't too old to defend a woman's honor."

"Whoa, boys," Granddaddy cautioned. "No need to get your blood boilin'."

Coosie laughed until he coughed. "Shoot, Pop, anything that gets blood boilin' at my age is good. Sorry, Thad."

Thad waved his thumbless hand. "Forget it. Sometimes we act like brothers."

"I thought we was brothers," Shorty said.

In the silence, I studied each of their eyes.

"Shorty's right," Quirt added. "We can bicker and fight, but we'll stand with each other in the tough times. That's what matters."

"Well, who wants to stand with me and go

over to the Round-Up for a sandwich?" Bronc reached down and pulled Coosie to his feet.

Grandpa stood. "Come on, Little Brother."

I glanced down at the lobby table. "I got to stay here and watch Miss Diane's box. I promised I'd keep it safe."

"Boys, I'm goin' to pass too," Quirt Payton insisted. "My stomach's been actin' up today."

"Do you know somethin' we don't?" Shorty asked.

"My brain don't know anything, but maybe my guts knows. Anyway, all the food would look good, and I'd just eat and get sick. Reckon I'll stay here with Little Brother and guard the junk jewelry."

"Think I'll go have me a piece of hot apple pie with cheese melted over it," Grandpa said.

"Little Brother, your granddaddy is an amazing man. I've known him for sixty years and he eats twice as much as anyone else, yet stays twice as skinny. How does he do that?" Coosie asked.

"Grandma says he must have tapeworms that visit at night and eat up all the excess," I explained.

Coosie gave me that man-in-the-moon grin. "Maybe Katie is right."

"Quirt, can we bring you back anything?" Thad offered.

"An Alka-Seltzer," he replied.

"You got it, huh?" Shorty said.

"Yep."

"You listen to the ol' marshal, Little Brother," Shorty continued. "Some folks have joints that can predict the weather. Quirt has a stomach that predicts trouble."

"Really?"

"Probably not." Shorty patted my shoulder. "But sometimes it seems that way."

We watched as Bronc led Coosie, Thad, Shorty, and Granddaddy out the front door of the Matador.

I opened the cigar box and fingered the contents.

"You ought to take inventory, Little Brother," Quirt said.

"What do you mean?"

"Get a pencil and paper and make a list of ever'thin' in the box. If it ends up being stolen goods, you'll have a record."

I glanced over at the empty registration desk. "You think Miss Diane would care?"

"Of course not. You'd be lookin' after her, sort of protectin' her reputation."

"How's that?"

"No one could complain that she stole somethin', if you had a list of what was in there." Quirt sat back and folded his hands. "I learned that lesson the hard way."

I sat back just like him. "What happened?"

"I was jist a kid, barely turned twenty and took

a job as deputy to Marshal Wiley Barnes down in Orogrande, Dona Anna Country. Ol' Wiley was meaner than most of the outlaws in that day, and a pretty fair shot with a pistol. No one ever escaped from one of Wiley's jails when he was around."

"They never tried?"

"They never tried twice."

"Did he shoot them?"

Quirt's eyebrows revealed the answer. "I was on the job about a week, mainly arrestin' drunks, footpads and sneakthieves."

"Footpad and sneakthief?"

"Burglars and pickpockets. I pulled jail duty when Wiley kicked open the door and shoved in the biggest man I've ever seen in my life. He'd make Bronc look like a dwarf. Wiley had him handcuffed. He hollered, 'This is Tiny Edwards . . . sack up his belongings, make a list for him to sign, and then put him in cell Number 3. Whatever you do, don't take off them wrist-irons. I'm goin' after his big brother.' "

"A bigger brother?"

"For the life of me, I didn't know how to get things out of his ducking trouser pockets without unshacklin' his hands."

"So what did you do?"

"I yanked off his boots to make sure he wasn't totin' a sneak gun or a hideaway knife, then slapped a leg iron to his ankle and the other end to the bed. He emptied his pockets on the floor, then flopped on the jail bed and went sound to sleep."

"If he went to sleep wearin' leg irons, he must have been awful tired," I said.

"He had spent most of the day in a Chinese Jos House."

"What's that?"

"Opium, Little Brother."

"But that's illegal."

"Not in those days. Besides, Tiny was the type that never paid much attention to details of the law. I sacked up his goods but didn't make a list. He wasn't in a mood to sign nothin'."

"Did you put the handcuffs back on him?"

"You see, Little Brother, you are already a better lawman than I was back then. I surmised the leg irons would hold him, what with the jail cell locked. Besides, he could crush my skull in his hands. I didn't want to go back in there."

"What happened next?"

"I heard a ruckus out in the street. I peeked out the door in time to witness Tiny's brother, Francis, pick up Marshal Wiley over his head and toss him in the stock tank in front of the hardware. Them Edwards boys was huge. Not as huge as their mama, but they was huge. I took off to stop Francis from drownin' the marshal." Quirt paused and loosened his tie.

I leaned forward. "What did you do?"

"I shot him three times . . . sort of."

"How do you sort of shoot someone three times?"

"I jumped on his back and slammed the barrel of my Colt on his head a couple times."

"You tried to cold-cock him?"

"Most men would go down on the first blow. I was gettin' a tad worried when I slammed it down a third time. He growled like a black bear wakin' up for the spring. He tossed me to the dirt like I was a gunnysack of walnuts, grabbing at my gun as I hit the ground. I knew if I let go of my gun, I'd be dead. Twenty ain't a age you want to die, Little Brother. So, I didn't turn loose."

"What happened then?"

"I squeezed the trigger tryin' to get control of my gun. That .44 blasted away."

"That's when you shot him three times?"

"I only fired one bullet."

"But you said you shot him three times."

"Sort of shot him three times. Later on, Doc Brackson figured it out."

"Dr. Brackson is Grandma's doctor," I said.

"No, that's his son. This was ol' man Brackson. He told me that the bullet tore into Francis's wrist, hit a bone, deflected into his shoulder where it hit his collarbone and came out the back of his shoulder and struck his head behind his ear."

"Did you kill him?"

"Nope. By the time the bullet hit his head it was purdy much spent. It just knocked him out and left him with three wounds. Word got around that I was so fast with pulling the trigger that I had shot him three times and it sounded like a single shot, a reputation that ain't bad to have. Made some hombres think twice before pullin' a gun on me."

"So, you saved the marshal?"

"I suppose I did, but it cost me."

"How's that?"

"Well, the marshal was dryin' off when someone from the hardware hollered that Tiny Edwards was running down the alley draggin' the whole dadgum bedframe."

"How did he get out of jail?"

"Kicked a hole in the wall. A big hole."

"He pulled out the whole bed?"

"Just the bedframe. He left the mattress," Quirt explained.

"Did you catch him?"

"Oh, yeah."

"How did that cost you?"

"He was in jail for a month. When the opium wore off, he wasn't much trouble. Naturally, he wanted his goods."

"You put them in the envelope?"

"Yeah, but there was no list. Tiny insisted he had a double-eagle. That was a twenty-dollar gold coin, Little Brother."

"You couldn't find it?"

"He didn't have a dime. But he pitched such a fit, I gave him a double-eagle. That was my first month's pay."

I trotted over to the front counter and retrieved a pencil and paper. I was not about to let those contents be uninventoried.

CHAPTER 39

The silver-plated broach held twelve green stones. Even as a kid, I was sure they weren't genuine. I pushed back my straw, cowboy hat. "Mr. Payton, where do they get the cut glass they put in jewelry?"

The retired lawman lounged in the leather chair, his back to the wall and studied the front door of the Matador Hotel. "Little Brother, you and me is pards, so I reckon you can call me Quirt."

I couldn't hold back the grin. "You're the only one I know by the name of Quirt."

"Aren't you goin' to ask me how I got that name?" Quirt sat up straight and rubbed his stomach.

I held a dangling, red-glass earring above my head so the chandelier light reflected through it. "Granddaddy said it was none of my business, that a cowboy doesn't ask about names."

"Pop is a good man, one of the finest Christian men I've ever met. We always felt that if we had Pop on the crew, the Good Lord was lookin' after us. But did he mention it's alright for a man to tell you about his name if he chooses to?"

I laid down the earring and recorded it on my paper. "Yes, sir, he did."

Quirt glanced at me from time to time, but kept focused on the front door. "I grew up as a lad in Victoria, Texas. I was the youngest of six boys. My daddy called me the Little Whippersnapper. Back then, I was small for my age. My brothers took up the name and by the time I reached school, they were callin' me Whip. But the boys in the fourth grade teased a lot with that name."

I sorted the jewelry by colors. "Why is that?"

"They all decided since my name was Whip, they needed to whip me. Well, I came home one day with busted knuckles and . . ."

I rubbed a purple ring across the glass. "Busted knuckles?" It left no scratch.

"I said they 'tried' to whip me. Most were unsuccessful. I complained to my daddy about my nickname. He said, 'Son, we won't call you Whip anymore.' Then he looked around the barn and spied a leather strap. 'We'll call you Quirt.' A quirt is a short ridin' whip. The name stuck."

"I like the name." I held up the green broach. "This one looks like chips of glass from a 7-Up bottle."

"It's a shame they wasted a good bottle." He chuckled, then grabbed his midsection. "I reckon I shouldn't laugh. I hurt too much. You didn't ask me my Christian name."

"No, sir. I can't ask that either. Granddaddy

would make me stay at home if I embarrassed him like that." As I recollect, there were five red, five green, five blue, two amber, two purple and six clear glass jewels. I might be wrong on some of the numbers, except the clear glass ones. I remember that for sure.

He leaned real close and whispered, "My name is Horace."

I put my hand over my mouth and coughed. To keep from grinning, I chewed on my tongue.

"But don't you dare tell anyone that."

"No, sir, I won't." I couldn't believe both he and Coosie had the same first name, and they hadn't ever told each other. I plucked up an amber-colored pair of earrings. I drug them across the glass table. "Look at these, I think they were made out of an old cough medicine bottle."

A truck backfired on the street. Quirt's hand dropped to his holstered gun. "Little Brother, did you ever see a gravesite covered with broken glass?"

"No. Why did they do that? Someone could hurt themselves." I finished the purples and started recording the red jewelry.

"They put an iron or wood border around the plot, then covered the entire area with broken glass from bottle and jars. It can be a beautiful sight if you catch the sun reflectin' through them. But the reason it's done is to keep the wolves and coyotes from diggin' up the body and chewin' on a man's bones."

I dropped a clear-glass, gold ring on the table. "Wolves and coyotes eat dead bodies?"

"As long as it ain't been dead a long time."

I folded my arms across my chest. The tin badge rub against my arm. "That makes my stomach hurt."

"It probably don't hurt as bad as mine." Quirt's face looked sunken, more ancient than one of the bit players in a Saturday western serial.

"Has your stomach always hurt like that?"

"Far back as I can remember. I always knew the day I was goin' to catch up with the *malo hombre* I was trailin'. There was a horse thief out of Raton called Walker Fritz. He'd come over to Rio Arriba County and steal horses, sell them in Colorado, then hide out in the Raton area. I started trailin' him in Brazos, followed him all the way up to Pagosa Springs, Colorado. I had to keep my distance and wait for him to get back into New Mexico to arrest him. So I followed him for about three weeks. He disappeared the day we rode back down to Raton."

"What do you mean, disappeared?" I logged the green jewelry on my borrowed paper.

"In the midst of Raton Pass he just up and vanished, horse and all. He must have known I was followin' him."

I slipped a green ring on my finger. "What did you do?"

194

"I figured two could play that game. So I up and disappeared too."

"You did?" I tugged at the ring, but it wouldn't come off.

"I cut back into the boulders and covered my tracks. I figured that Walker would hide in the boulders somewhere until he saw me ride by, and then he would go off to his hideout."

"But he didn't see you ride by." I yanked on the ring so hard, my hat tumbled to the floor, but it finally slipped off.

"Exactly. I might not know where he was, but he didn't know where I was either. I figured if I waited it out, he would come lookin' for me."

I scooped up my hat and tossed the ring in the cigar box. "But you covered your tracks. How could he find you?"

"Horse thieves are good at trackin', and ol' Walker was one of the best."

"How long did you have to wait?" After rubbing my finger some, I continued my inventory.

"Five days."

"You sat in the rocks and waited for five days?"

"Sometimes a man has to have patience. But it was a strain. I ran out of drinkin' water after three days, and on the mornin' of the fifth, I was plannin' on ridin' down out of there. But I woke up with a stomachache."

"Because you hadn't had any water?"

"Nope. It was a nervousness that comes before

a battle, and I knew that Walker was ridin' in. I think of it as a God-given survival instinct."

"You think God gives that to everyone?"

"I think we all get different things, and this is what He gave me."

"Quirt, do you believe in God?"

"Yes, I do, Little Brother. Your granddaddy made sure of that several years back. Do you?"

"Yes, sir. I was baptized last year."

Quirt pulled off his glasses and laid them on the table. "I probably ought to get myself baptized one of these days."

"So your stomach hurt that day you were waitin' for Walker?"

"Somethin' fierce."

"Like right now?"

"Sort of similar."

"What did you do?" I finished my list and double-checked the box full of jewelry to see if I had missed anything.

"I built a breakfast fire, although I didn't have any food left. Then I stuck my hat on a stick and raised it behind some boulders and waited."

"Did he shoot your hat?"

"Five times. Walker Fritz was a cautious man. As soon as I heard his gun empty-click, I stood and challenged him to throw down or die."

I pulled the big, clear, glass-looking ring out of the box and studied it. "What did he do?"

"He threw down, of course. A man with an

empty gun don't put up much of a struggle."

"Whatever happened to him?"

"Turns out he was wanted in El Paso for killin' a couple of card dealers. The Texans sentenced him to fifty years in jail."

"When was that?"

"About forty-five years ago."

"So, he's still in prison?"

"Maybe. He could have gotten the sentence shortened for good behavior. Provided he lived that long."

"Then he could be out of prison now?"

"That's a thought that keeps me awake some nights."

Quirt Payton pulled his revolver when the front door of the Matador Hotel jingled open.

CHAPTER 40

The two men in white T-shirts that had blustered in looking for Leon Herbert now marched over to the front desk.

"I knew it," Quirt mumbled.

"Trouble?"

"Back me up, Little Brother." Quirt Payton swung to his feet.

The words "back me up" made the hair on the back of my neck flare. I stood, but was too frozen to move. What was a kid with cap guns supposed to do?

The taller of the two banged on the bell next to the registry.

Quirt put his hand on my shoulder. "Just wait," he whispered.

"Shelby, we've got to get out of town," the short one whined.

"Not until we get our money."

"Is this goin' to work?"

I glanced down at my shirt. I unpinned my U.S. Deputy Marshal's badge and shoved it in Quirt's hand.

The tall one, Shelby, banged on the bell again.

"Hey, anyone back there?"

Quirt and me inched our way closer when Miss Diane came out of the back room. I saw him pin my badge on the inside of his suit coat. We stayed behind a huge, plaster-coated pillar that blocked our view from theirs.

"Who are you?" the shorter one asked.

"Are you looking for a room?" she asked. "We need cash in advance."

"Is that a proposition?" the shorter one sneered.

Miss Diane turned back to the office.

"We're lookin' for Diane, eh . . . Andrews," Shelby announced.

She turned back. "I'm Diane Anderson."

I peeked around to see the shorter one lean across the desk. "Are you Leon Herbert's girl-friend?"

She brushed blonde bangs out of her eyes. "If you are friends of Leon's, I don't have any idea where he is . . . and I don't care."

"Get up on the oak chair, Little Brother," Quirt whispered and pointed to a straight-back chair against the pillar.

I climbed up and it made me a little taller than him.

"You need to step outside with me and Painter, so we can ask you a few questions," Shelby growled at Miss Diane.

"I'm not going anywhere with you."

He flung himself across the counter and grabbed her arm. "Like Hades, you aren't. You're goin' to lead us to Leon and you're goin' to do it right now."

"Stay behind the pillar," Quirt whispered.

199

"Turn loose of me!" Miss Diane shouted.

Quirt stepped out into the middle of the lobby. "She said, turn loose!"

When they spun around, Painter brandished a long-bladed knife in his hand.

"Who in blazes are you?" Shelby grumbled.

Quirt flashed my badge. "Deputy U.S. Marshal, Quirt Payton. Put down the knife, son."

"I didn't see that badge close up, old man," he snarled. "You're jist one of them ol' men playin' cribbage."

"Maybe you can see this close up." Quirt yanked out his single-action revolver and pointed it right at the one with the knife.

"He's got a gun!" Painter shouted.

When Shelby released Miss Diane, he had in his hand a Colt 1911 semi-auto pistol. "Now we both got a gun."

"Lay down the gun and knife, boys. I need to take you to the county jail and question you about a hold-up and shooting on 32nd Street."

"You ain't takin' us nowhere," Shelby snarled. "Now, back on out of here or you're dead."

"Mister, I've shot more men than you are years old. I won't mind addin' two more." I never heard Quirt growl like that before. There was no doubt in my ten-year-old mind that he would pull the trigger.

"I can hit you from here." Shelby waved the semi-auto across the lobby.

"You'd better hope you can," Quirt said. "Your partner will be dead by then, because my gun is aimed at his head, and I have never missed this close."

"I don't think he's bluffin'." Painter dropped his knife on the counter.

"Pick up that knife!" Shelby hollered.

"I'm unarmed, mister, you can't shoot me," the shorter one whined.

"We'll let the inquest decide that."

"I ain't jokin', old man!" Shelby screamed. "You don't back off, you're dead and I walk out the door."

"You're forgettin' one thing." Quirt nodded his head toward the pillar.

"What's that?"

"My partner."

"There ain't no one else in this room," Shelby said.

"Just because you can't see them, don't mean they aren't there. Partner, without exposin' yourself to being shot at, poke that .44 of yours around the corner."

I yanked out one of my cap guns, then froze.

"If either makes a dash for the door, blast them."

I held my cap gun out in front of me, and slowly inched it around the post, making sure I was out of sight.

"There is someone back there," Painter cried out, his hands still in the air.

"Probably just another of them old men."

"That gun don't look old," Painter said.

"Put your gun on the floor and slide it this way. Now!"

I peeked just enough to see Shelby lay the black, semi-auto pistol at his feet.

"I said, slide it this way."

Shelby glanced over at Painter, then nodded. He then kicked the gun across the lobby towards the stairwell. I was shocked as Quirt lowered his gun and trotted toward the handgun.

As soon as he did, the two broke for the front door.

"Don't fire, deputy!" Quirt shouted at me. "You might hit a bystander!"

The two were out the door when Quirt strolled back to the counter where Miss Diane bit her lip and shook her head.

"Didn't you know that was a diversion?" I complained. "The same thing happened to the Cisco Kid last week in Loredo."

"I knew it was, Little Brother. I didn't want to capture them. What was I going to do with them? Just wanted to chase them off."

Miss Diane shook her head. "I can't believe what I just witnessed."

"That an old man and a kid just chased off a couple of punks?" Quirt asked.

"You could have been shot," she said.

"They aren't the shootin' type," Quirt replied.

I stared out the front door at people walking by on the sidewalk. "I thought the policeman said they shot a clerk over on 32nd Street."

"I'm sure they did. There is one type, Little Brother, that will shoot an unarmed person. There is another type that will shoot when they have a gun pointed back at them. They weren't that type."

When Quirt shoved his gun back in his holster, I tucked my cap gun back in mine. "Little Brother did good, didn't he, Miss Diane?"

She folded her arms across her chest. "Yes, he's growing taller in my eyes, that's for sure."

I felt my face heat up. "Oh, no, Miss Diane. I was just standin' on the chair."

CHAPTER 41

Shorty swaggered into the Matador first. They all sported toothpicks except for Coosie, who chomped on an unlit cigar. Me and Quirt Payton held cards and stared at the cribbage board when they returned, but that was just for show. We visited with Miss Diane, and when she went to the office to call Detective Tyler Young to report the confrontation, we plopped down on the big, brown couches.

"You two look half-asleep," Bronc said. "You should have come with us to the Round-Up Café for coffee."

"The peach cobbler was first rate," Thad Brewer added. "Boys, I reckon I've had peach cobbler at the Round-Up ever' Wednesday since FDR was president."

When Bronc landed on the sofa next to me, I shot up in the air about a foot.

"Some day," Shorty declared, bent, wooden toothpick in his mouth, "Gretchen is goin' to retire as pie cook and then where will we be?"

"Some of us will be permanently retired long before that," Coosie mumbled. "If you catch my drift."

I stared over at Granddaddy.

"Oh, don't worry, Little Brother," Quirt chimed

in. "Pop's got a good twenty years before he catches up with ol' Coosie."

"You young boys can tease," Coosie said, "but at my age, ever' day is a gift from above."

"Dyin's not the worst thing that could happen to a man," Quirt said.

Shorty picked at his crooked, white teeth. "There's been a few times in my life I'd have to agree. That time I busted my back, when that sorrel blew up on me and tossed me over the edge of Verde Canyon. I laid there on the rocks for two whole days wishin' I would die. When that old wolf trapper wandered along, I begged him to shoot me. Is that what you mean?"

Quirt nodded. "It's part of it."

"I'll tell you when I wanted to die," Bronc said. "I shot a little girl one time. Dyin' would have been better than that."

"What happened?" I asked.

"A couple of them Peach Grove boys came into Gallup, got drunk, and told ever'one in town they was goin' to shoot me on sight."

"Which ones of them boys?" Thad asked. "They was all mean."

"The one with curly red hair . . ."

"That's Perry. He got killed over at Lincoln," Quirt announced.

"I thought it was Ezekiel," Shorty said.

Thad tugged on his tight, shirt collar. "It was both of them."

Coosie pulled the unlit cigar out of his mouth. "In the hotel fire?"

"Perry died 'cause of gunshot wounds. They say Ezekiel drunk himself under a table and died from the smoke of that fire," Quirt explained.

"I didn't know that," Thad said. "I seen Charlie Peach last spring at the horse sale down in Socorro."

"It was Perry and Micah that hounded me," Bronc said.

"Did you ever notice that the taller them Peach boys was, the nicer he was? Charlie was the tallest. Micah and Perry were the shortest," Thad added.

"What do you mean by that?" Shorty demanded.

"I'm just sayin', the taller ones was the nicest. It ain't a general statement about all mankind, just one way to tell them twelve Peach Grove boys apart."

"I had told Marshal Duncan that a couple of them Peach Grove boys stole cattle off the Anchor-Bar-4 and they didn't take kindly to it," Bronc continued. "So they stalked me. When I heard they were at the feed mill, I hiked over to confront them about it. I had just stepped up on the boardwalk when a shot blasted through the store window in front of me. I dove flat, my gun drawn. I figured they would charge out of there firin'."

"But they didn't?" I asked.

Bronc stared down at his boots. His voice softened. "Perry shoved a little Mexican girl out the door in front of them."

"And you shot her?" I gasped.

"Little Brother, for years I'd wake up in the middle of the night tryin' to take that bullet back. The best I could do was jerk my gun down a little. Hit her in both legs with one slug." Bronc slumped back against the brown couch and closed his eyes. "I can see them terrified, brown eyes to this day."

"What happened to the Peach Grove boys?" Shorty asked.

"They slipped out the back alley and disappeared before the marshal showed up."

"Did you get arrested?" I asked.

"I should have been tossed in jail, but things was different back then, dependin' on what town you were in, whether Mexicans got a fair shake. They ruled it an accident. Said she got hit in the crossfire, since I had been shot at first. But I knew different."

"What happened to the girl, Bronc?" Granddaddy asked.

"I paid for the doc to take out the bullet. One leg had permanent damage. The other, with the spent lead, healed in time."

"Is she still alive?" I asked.

"I don't know. She and her folks moved over here to Duke City so she could learn to walk again. I'd stop by ever' year around Christmas time and leave her a card and a twenty-dollar gold piece, but her daddy wouldn't let me see her. That's okay, of course. I don't think I could have looked in them eyes. One winter they was gone. The neighbors reported they moved to San Louis Obispo, California. I never kept up, but if she's still alive, she's limpin' bad and hurtin'. It's because of me. I ain't never forgive myself for that. I would rather have died that day, than to live with the memory."

"How come you never told us that story before, Bronc?" Thad asked.

"There is some things a man can hardly admit. But I reckon Judgment Day will reveal 'em all."

"None of us is lookin' forward to that day," Coosie added.

"Except for Pop," Quirt chided.

"Do you remember that time Pop backed down Bill Ortiz and that bunch down in Lordsburg?" Coosie asked.

"Pop, did you ever tell Little Brother about that?" Shorty pressed.

"Now, boys, don't embarrass me in front of my grandson. He thinks I spent most of my life bein' a carpenter."

"I'll tell him," Shorty said. " 'Cause I ain't never seen anything like it."

"I reckon any of us could tell the story," Quirt added. "We was all there, except for Thad."

"I was freightin' hay for ol' Tom McKennon that year," Thad Brewer declared. "He still hasn't paid me that bonus he offered."

"McKennon never paid anyone that bonus. He used that line jist to recruit suckers," Bronc hooted.

"You know what? He retired a rich man down in Yuma and built a big house along the Colorado River," Quirt said. "But he died huntin' ducks. I heard he tripped over some rocks and blasted himself with that fine English over-and-under."

"Both barrels?" Coosie said.

Bronc shrugged. "I don't reckon it mattered much about that."

"But what about Granddaddy and Bill Ortiz?" I prodded.

The tap of a lady's heels on the wooden-floor lobby centered our attention on Miss Diane. "I suppose Little Brother has told you how he and the marshal saved me from great harm?"

"He did what?" Granddaddy boomed.

"And he's modest, too. Detective Young will be over later this afternoon to get a statement from Marshal Quirt and Little Brother." She pirouetted and clicked back to the office.

Coosie pulled out his chawed cigar and turned to Quirt. "What's this about?"

Quirt flashed my badge, still pinned to his coat. "You tell 'em, Little Brother. It's about time a cowboy like you had a chance to tell your own story."

CHAPTER 42

I must not have been too good at chronicling the excitement, because Quirt interrupted me at least a dozen times. But I have to admit, it felt good. For the first time all afternoon, the story was about me, and I had the attention and respect of a half-dozen, old-time cowboys. I enjoyed it as long as I could.

"I told you the minute he came walkin' through the front door of the Matador that the boy was a fine cowboy," Shorty bragged. "It's in the eyes, ain't it?"

Coosie nodded his round, pumpkin head. When he chewed on the cigar, he reminded me of the bobble-head, ceramic doll of Winston Churchill that my granddaddy used to have on his back porch.

"I still want to hear the story about Grand-daddy and Bill Ortiz," I insisted when Quirt and I ran out of steam.

That's all the prod Shorty needed. "By the time we was in Lordsburg, ol' Bill Ortiz had settled down quite a bit. In his younger days, he terror-ized both sides of the border. But when we was there, he had a fairly nice spread south of the Pyramid Mountains."

"Ortiz was related to DelNorte, wasn't he?" Thad said.

"Yeah, his sister married DelNorte, but don't get started on DelNorte tales. Little Brother would be grown up before we could finish," Shorty declared. "Anyway, it's mighty parched country down in the bootheel, but ol' Bill had several springs and tanks that never seem to dry up."

Bronc ran strong fingers through his thin, gray hair. "We rode down to Lordsburg, then cut over to Hachita. Scoop Randall bought twelve Mexican bulls and wanted us to drive 'em back to Reserve."

"It took five of you to drive twelve bulls?" I asked.

"If we hadn't all been top hands, we never could of done it. They was a mean lot," Coosie said.

"He said they was too wild to put in a train car. I reckon he was right about that," Shorty laughed. "Remember that one-horned bull that almost leveled the Trails End Saloon at Aqua Caliente?"

"That's the maddest I ever seen a bartender," Coosie chuckled. "He acted like we wanted that bull to follow us through the door."

"Did you boys ever see the lobby of the Palace Hotel in Ft. Peer after them buffaloes got through with it? Now there was a mess," Bronc said.

211

"I heard they burnt it to the ground rather than repair it," Shorty added.

"What about Grandpa?" I whined. "What happened to him and Ortiz?"

Shorty patted my shoulder. "When we rode into Hachita, them bulls was in a stone corral that looked like a dadgum Spanish fort. Pop, how tall would you say them walls were?"

"A good ten feet," Granddaddy said. "I stood in my saddle and they came up to my nose. That was the tallest stone corral I ever saw."

I tried to imagine Grandpa standin' in the saddle. How I would have liked to see him in his prime.

"Speakin' of Stone Corral," Coosie paused for a deep, chest-rattling cough. "Did I tell you boys the time I met John Sontag out in California?"

"Don't change stories, Coosie," Quirt insisted.

"We stayed in Lordsburg a little too long and got down there about dark," Bronc said. "Two guards stood at the corral gate. They said there was some paperwork to settle up on, and that Bill Ortiz would ride to town in the mornin' and straighten it out."

"In them days, Little Brother, Hachita was still the wildest dive in New Mexico," Shorty replied. "We was plannin' on campin' out in the hills, 'cause there wasn't nobody in town you could turn your back on. But them guards told us Ortiz had rented us rooms and paid for supper in town. So we wanted to be hospitable, and took him up on it."

"He rented one room for the five of us, but the café served good food." Quirt stared at the front door. "We decided the safest thing to do in Hachita was to stay awake all evenin'."

"We should have been suspect when they said Bill paid for all the mescal we could drink," Bronc said. "But, your granddaddy . . . not bein' a drinkin' man, kept a watch on us. Me and Shorty danced with the girls before long, and ol' Coosie fell asleep at the table."

"You know me, boys, I take two swigs and I'm gone," Coosie muttered.

"I got into a card game with a horse doctor who was so good at cheatin' at cards, I kept playin' just to marvel at his skill," Quirt admitted.

"Was that Dr. Simmerman?" Thad asked.

"I think his name was Summerman," Quirt corrected. "He got shot in the throat in Silver City and went around several years with that bullet lodged in his Adam's apple."

I tried to swallow, but I felt a painful lump in my own throat.

"That explains why we wasn't in very good shape the next mornin'," Shorty said. "So, Ortiz shows up and tells us the Mexicans changed their minds and sold the bulls to him. We showed him the bill-of-sale and how Scoop done paid for them, but he says it's no good. Then he offers to pay us what Scoop had paid for the bulls."

"That meant he would be double-payin' for the bulls and we knowed ol' Ortiz better than that," Coosie chimed in.

Shorty tugged on his handlebar mustache. "We couldn't figure his game. So we told him we was supposed to bring them bulls to the ranch, and that's what we intended to do. Meanwhile, ol' Bronc didn't like the tone of things. 'Let's take 'em,' he declared. 'If anyone tries to stop us, we'll shoot 'em.' "

Bronc leaned over the chair and spit in the brass spittoon. "We was gettin' paid to herd them bulls. I didn't figure there was anything else to do."

Shorty's hands flailed as if orchestrating each word. "Now, Hachita don't need no excuse to get riled, but suddenly Ortiz had the whole dadgum town backin' up his hand. About a hundred guns drew to our five."

"And Ortiz claimed that he wouldn't give us a penny 'cause we treated him so poorly," Quirt added.

"I figured it was time to settle up with the Good Lord," Coosie admitted.

Bronc plopped his massive hand on my knee. "Courage has to be tempered with wisdom, Little Brother. We'd have backed off and pondered a different plan, but Pop was insistent."

214

Shorty stared me right in the eyes. "Your grand-daddy stormed up to Ortiz, nose to nose, both of them with guns drawn. He said, 'Bill, you ain't treatin' us square. We came for them bulls. They legally belong to Scoop Randall and you know it. So, I reckon that's what we're goin' to do.'"

My head spun as Coosie spoke. "Ortiz growled, 'El Diablo, you will, Pop. I'll shoot you before you get to the gate if you try to take my bulls.'"

I could barely speak. "What did you do, Granddaddy?"

Granddaddy rubbed his clean-shaven chin. "I was young and opinionated, Little Brother. I had to do what was right."

Quirt then explained, "Pop said, 'Bill, you pull the trigger and you and I will both die today. As for me . . . I'm only one step away from heaven and I'm anxious to see what it's like. My mama and daddy's there already, as well as the sweetest sister a man ever had. Some days I get to missin' them a lot. So if you pull that trigger, you'd just be sendin' me to glory. But where will you go, Bill? Did you ever ponder what you are one step away from?' Ortiz roared back at him, 'You're crazy, Pop. Them bulls aren't worth dying for.'"

Shorty jumped in when Quirt took a breath. "Your granddaddy said, 'I was hired to do a job. If a man can't be trusted to do a job, he ain't worth much. So I'll do my job, and you do yours,

Bill. And we'll let the Lord judge things. How's that?' "

"Then Pop rode straight for the corral," Quirt said. "Me and the boys hurried to mount and ride with him. Ortiz and the whole town was on foot, runnin' alongside, pointing their guns at us the whole way."

"I learned to pray that day, boys," Shorty admitted. "I jist kept sayin', 'Lord, if you come for Pop, how about takin' the rest of us too?' "

"The guards threw carbines to their shoulders," Bronc declared. "But Pop waved them off and opened the gate."

"I truly expected ol' Bill to shoot, which would have been a signal to the others," Quirt admitted.

"So did I, boys," Granddaddy replied.

"But it got quiet," Bronc continued. "Only Crazy Alice mumblin' to herself, like she always did. Ever'one else was just holdin' his breath and watchin'."

Coosie raised his hand as if askin' for a turn. "Someone from town hollered, 'Bill, ain't you goin' to shoot them?' "

Then Shorty chimed in. "Ortiz said, 'Nope.' "

And Bronc picked it up. " 'How come?' someone else shouted."

"I can still hear Ortiz's words," Quirt said. " ' 'Cause I know what it's like to have a sweet sister. I don't aim to disappoint her today.' "

Coosie shook his head. "Bill just turned and mounted that black stallion of his and rode south."

"And we pushed them wild bulls north as fast as they would trot," Shorty added.

Bronc sighed. "I didn't feel safe until we crossed the railroad tracks."

"I ain't never forgot them words, Pop," Quirt said. "I'd never met a man anxious to get to heaven."

"Personally, I'm not all that anxious to face judgment," Bronc replied.

CHAPTER 43

Grandpa pulled off his gold, wire-framed spectacles and rubbed the bridge of his long, thin nose. I knew he was goin' to preach a little. So I opened the lid of the cigar box and studied the fake jewels.

"I recollect me and Shorty sittin' in the saddle and listenin' to Christmas carols sung at that one room church on the outskirts of Hobbs. We spent half the night talkin' about Jesus . . ."

"I ain't never forgot that, Pop," Shorty said.

"I remember Quirt comin' to terms with the Lord, when he had found that cancer. But for the rest of you, I've told you about Jesus and I've prayed for you, so I reckon that's all I can do. At times I feel like a failure, but each of us is accountable for ourselves, so I need to let it go at that."

"Pop, you know our past," Thad said. "It ain't purdy."

"Yep, and that's why I'm tellin' you it ain't too late for any of you."

"Pop, do you remember that Winchester 1873 carbine that we dug out of the crickbed at the base of that mountain near Clayton?" Bronc said.

"It wasn't much of a gun," Granddaddy replied.

"That's my point," Bronc continued. "It was the rustiest gun I ever saw. Me and Pop dug it out by hand so careful as if it was a valuable treasure. The wood was gone, of course, but the metal was there. It was a First Model with mortised dust cover and no safety on the lever. So we pondered on all the gunfights it must have seen and who might have carried it. It was the rustiest piece of metal I'd ever seen in my life. We even considered givin' it to the cowboy museum in Lincoln. I went to hand it over to Pop, and it slipped out of my hand."

"When that rusty thing hit the campfire rocks, it shattered as if it were made of thin glass," Granddaddy said.

"For a while we just stared at the pile of rust that used to be a gun. Then Pop pulled off his Stetson and held it over his heart. 'From dust it came and to dust it will return,' he said." Bronc grinned and shook his head. "It was way beyond help. Wasn't nothin' left to do but kick dirt over it. Well, Pop, I don't know about the other boys, but that's me. Too much has gone on in my life. Each one of them sins just eats away at me until there's nothin' left redeemable. Ain't much left to do but kick a little dirt over me."

I listened to the air-slapping noise of the overhead fan. Somewhere out on Central Avenue a car honked. I felt as uncomfortable as sitting in the front row at a tent-revival meeting.

Granddaddy stretched his long legs in front of him, and I reckon that was the first time I noticed how slick the knees of his wool trousers had become. "Bronc, your story is almost right. But let me set it straight. You boys ain't Winchester '73s."

"Shoot, when Coosie was born, there weren't no '73s," Shorty hooted.

"That's right," Granddaddy said. "The Creator made you better than that. I think, by comparison, you're more like a Winchester 1866."

"What do you mean, Pop?" Coosie asked.

"Did you ever dig up a '66, boys?" Granddaddy said.

"Not that I remember," Thad Brewer declared.

"The wood's gone, just like the '73. And the barrel is, at best, good for nothin' more than a tent peg. Ah, but the receiver. It's tarnish dark-green, but that brass don't rust. You buff that receiver up a bit and the mustard patina jumps right out at you. That gun can be rebuilt, and will last forever if it's taken care of. I reckon that's where you are. The Lord don't see you as goin' back to dirt, boys. He sees the shiny brass that he can polish up to new life."

"Are you goadin' us, Pop?" Shorty asked.

"If you feel prodded, Shorty, it's the shovel of the Lord. He's diggin' you up and intends on restorin' you. You don't have to clean up anything. That's His job. All you got to do is believe that Jesus is who He says He is, and did what He said He did."

"You're soundin' like my mama," Bronc said.

"What would your dear mama say, if she heard you were trustin' Jesus down here?" Granddaddy challenged.

A grin broke across Bronc's pockmarked face. "I reckon she would shout 'glory' up and down the streets of heaven."

"Are you dumpin' mama's guilt on us, Pop?" Coosie asked.

"No, boys, you are doin' that yourself. Don't do it for me, and don't even do it for your mama. She won't be able to stand by your side on judgment day. That's a trail we'll ride down all by ourselves. Do it because it's right. It's true. Just don't tell me lies about you bein' too far gone to redeem," Granddaddy insisted. "It just ain't so."

I listened to the twap-twap-twap of the ceilin' fan and noticed a couple of 'em wipe their eyes.

Quirt Payton busted out of the blanket of silence. "Well, dadgum it, Pop, why don't you just speak your mind and not beat around the bush?"

I never knew how many of them Grandpa reached with his message and his prayers, but I went with him a few years later when Shorty McGuire was baptized in a little, white-clapboard Baptist church east of town. A twenty-one–screen, motion-picture house stands there today.

I do know that Granddaddy would have kept pressin', but for the sounds of high heel shoes strutting across the lobby of the Matador Hotel.

"It's about four o'clock, boys. I guess I'll go see Leon at the Pit. If you want to tag along, that's fine. I think Detective Young will be coming by too. At least, that's what he said."

I jumped up and grabbed the cigar box full of jewelry. "I'm comin' with you, Miss Diane."

I imagined a musical lilt in her voice. "Little Brother, are you going to save me again?"

I chewed on my tongue and tipped my straw hat. "Yes, ma'am, I reckon I am."

CHAPTER 44

A warm rain drizzled on us as we filed out the back door of the Matador. Miss Diane insisted that I walk beside her under that black umbrella she toted. Looking back, it was only right that the lady and the little kid have the umbrella, but on that day I felt six-foot-tall. Up to that time, Daisy Mae, from the comics, *Lil' Abner*, had been the girl of my dreams. But for several years after, Miss Diane Anderson filled her fantasy role.

Quirt marched only a step back, his narrow eyes tracing every shadow and sound. Shorty tried to keep up with him, sometimes at a jog. From what I recollect, Thad and Bronc sauntered along discussing whose mother had been most devout. Grandpa lagged back with Coosie, who hadn't moved very fast since an encounter with a cougar in 1921.

In 1929, the Central New Mexico Cold Storage and Transfer had gone bankrupt, along with most of the state. The three-story, brick building served as a factory for army blankets during the war. Since 1946, it had squatted on the back street as a reminder of what used to be. The first-story windows and doors were long busted and boarded up. The second-story, and some of the third-story windows were also broken, jagged proof of an abandoned building.

The concrete ramps slanted down from the alley and leveled off so that a half-dozen Mack trucks could back up and load blankets at the same time. During a New Mexico downpour, the Pit filled up like a swimming pool, but the drizzle that day did little more than float leaves and trash to the storm drain.

Miss Diane stopped at the edge of the building. "Boys, I need you to wait here a few minutes. Detective Young wants to catch Leon down in the Pit. If you are all down there with me, he might drive on by. I don't care if I see him or not, but the detective thinks the only way to catch those other two is to nab Leon."

"I reckon Leon would talk. He don't look like the type to keep a secret if it caused him pain," Bronc remarked.

We huddled behind a row of huge, empty, wooden, wine barrels as Miss Diane, her blond, curly hair topped by a charcoal-grey hat, strutted down the concrete ramp. Her umbrella protected her from the drizzle.

Quirt organized the rest of us. "Thad and Bronc, sneak around the east side. You both packin' boot pistols?"

Bronc patted his pant cuff. "It ain't a sock full of money, that's for sure."

"You expectin' trouble, Quirt?" Shorty asked.

"The marshal expects trouble ever'day," Coosie hooted.

"Old man, you're packin' iron, so you and Pop stay here. Me and Shorty will take the west side . . . once he's down in the Pit, I'll slip around to the south."

"I should have gone up to the room and got my gun," Shorty griped.

"You can use one of mine," I offered.

"Take it," Quirt added. "He ain't goin' to come up that side if he sees a gun, and I guarantee ol' Leon don't know a cap gun from a potato. I'm goin' to use Little Brother's badge. We're not planning on shootin' anyone. Just want to box him in until the detective gets here."

"What about me?" I asked.

Quirt pointed at the box in my hand. "You stay out of the rain and guard the jewels. Sooner or later, I reckon you'll have to hand those over to Leon."

I hiked back with Grandpa and Coosie and kept concealed behind the barrels. I could peek out and see Miss Diane and her black umbrella at the bottom of the concrete ramp, but little else. Grandpa stood on my left, his posture erect. His worn, small-brimmed Stetson tilted just a little to the right.

Coosie leaned against a barrel next to him. With his big, floppy-brimmed, cowboy hat, I could hardly tell he was bald. "Pop, how long was we parked up Yucca Canyon waitin' for the rustlers?"

Granddaddy rubbed his narrow chin, but kept his eyes on the street. "Four days, I recollect."

Coosie drummed his fingers on the barrel. "Them was long days."

"But it was spring." Granddaddy tugged off his gold-framed glasses and rubbed his eyes. They squeaked when he rubbed them that way. "I enjoyed the rest."

I wondered what Miss Diane could be thinking, as she stood down there alone. "Did you catch some rustlers?" I asked.

"No, we caught butterflies," Coosie replied. "It seems the rustlers were on to us, and took the cattle right up over September Pass, which was quite a feat in August, let alone May. But some big, ol', orange, Mexican butterflies came swoopin' in."

"Giant Monarchs, Little Brother," Granddaddy said. "We tried to see who could catch the biggest."

Coosie yanked out his teeth and slipped them into his vest pocket. "Pop won. He caught an eleven-inch wingspan."

I tried to imagine a butterfly bigger than the cigar box.

"I've never seen anything like it," Coosie added.

"So, if Leon doesn't show up, we'll catch butterflies?" I asked.

Coosie pointed to the shadows behind the busted crates against the building. "Or rats."

I crept closer to the edge of the ramp and peered down at Miss Diane. Just when my mind flitted to foot-wide butterflies and foot-tall rodents, Leon appeared. I crouched behind the barrels. He glared up and down the street, then shuffled down the ramp towards Miss Diane. My hands and knees on damp concrete, I tilted my head so I could hear every word.

"Where are they?" Leon demanded.

Miss Diane folded the umbrella and rested it on her shoulder. "What are you talking about?"

"Girl, this isn't a time to joke. I need them right now."

She spun the closed umbrella. "I thought you gave them to me."

"Don't play this game!" he shouted. "You know I meant you to keep them safe."

"I believe you said someday they would be mine."

"Things didn't work out that way." He looked around. I dove behind the barrels. "Where are they?"

"Close by . . . but before I tell you where, I need you to answer a question. Why would you be so concerned about modern five-and-dime jewelry?"

"It's real!" he shouted.

She folded her arms across her chest. "Real what?"

Leon paced back and forth, his eyes darting toward the street. "Are you insultin' my dearly-departed mama?"

"Most of that jewelry can be purchased down the street at Woolsworth's right now. So, cut the crap, Leon."

He shoved a fist at her face. "I want that box of jewelry. I need to get out of town."

I glanced down at the White Owl cigar box. It felt a little damp, either from the drizzle or just nervous sweat.

Miss Diane backed away from Leon. "If giving them to you gets you on the road, I'll do that."

He grabbed her padded shoulder. "Don't worry, sweet thing. I'll call you from, eh, Tulsa."

She slapped his hand off with her umbrella. "I don't want to ever see you or talk to you again." She marched off towards us.

Leon followed her. "You're just sore because of Teresa. I'm just givin' her a lift to Lubbock, that's all. Her car broke down."

Brakes squealed from the street. Leon huddled behind Miss Diane. I glanced out expecting to see the detective storm down, but instead it was Shelby and Painter, with jeans jackets pulled over white T-shirts. I ducked down lower and glanced around, but couldn't see Grandpa or Coosie. In fact, I couldn't spot any of the old cowboys.

CHAPTER 45

Shelby stopped on the ramp, hands shoved in his coat pockets. "Well, if it ain't a double-crosser and his woman."

"I am not his woman. In fact, you three may do whatever you want. I'm leaving." Miss Diane headed up the ramp.

"You ain't goin' nowhere," Painter snapped.

Shelby bobbed his head up and down. "We want our ten-thousand dollars right now, Leon."

"Ten-thousand dollars?" Miss Diane choked. "Leon doesn't have a hundred dollars, let alone ten-thousand."

"He sure as Hades better have our ten grand." The shorter one, Painter, circled to the left.

Leon scooted around to keep Miss Diane between him and the two men. "If you had given me five more minutes, I would have had it."

"What do you mean, you would have had it?" Miss Diane questioned. "I don't have your ten-thousand dollars and you know it."

"You don't know nothin'," Leon growled.

"We gave you five more minutes, you'd be on Highway 66 headin' for Flagstaff," Painter insisted. "You told us that yourself."

"I thought you were goin' to Tulsa," Miss Diane replied.

"He and that dancin' girl was goin' to Los Angeles." Shelby eased down the ramp closer to Miss Diane. "Teresa was the one who told us to look for you over here."

Painter waved his knife. "Funny how much a woman will talk when she's scared her purdy face will be cut."

Miss Diane stood her ground. "You'll have to cut on Leon, because I don't have any idea what you are talking about. I want to leave."

Leon grabbed her arm. "Neither one of us is goin' to make it out of this concrete tomb if you don't give me that cigar box."

"You kept our ten grand in a cigar box?" Shelby barked. "You said you had a safe place for it."

Miss Diane jerked her arm away. "There isn't any money in that box."

"That jist shows how little you know. Where's the box?" Leon shouted.

"I'll have to go fetch it." She started to hike up the ramp.

Leon grabbed her arm again. "We'll all go fetch it."

"If she's got the box with our funds, we don't need Leon." Shelby pulled a gun and pointed it at Leon. "Say goodbye to your woman."

"Wait!" Leon shouted. "She has the box but she doesn't know where the funds are. They are disguised. You kill me and you'll never find them."

I figured right then that Quirt, Grandpa and the others would step forward, but I saw no movement. But when the short one moved at Miss Diane, brandishing his knife, I jumped up in front of the barrel.

"I've got the cigar box!" I shouted. I'd like to think that the words boomed out with power and confidence, but I probably squeaked like a scared jackrabbit.

"Who in blazes is the kid?" the tall one said.

Painter pointed his knife at me. "He was with them old men at the hotel."

"Give me the box, kid!" Leon shouted.

"Turn Miss Diane loose!" I hollered down at him.

"We ain't turnin' nobody loose!" Painter grabbed Miss Diane's arm.

I chewed on my tongue, too scared to move.

As if orchestrated by heaven's intervention, all six of the old men appeared, surrounding the loading ramp. Each cowboy hat pulled down tight, all but Grandpa toted a gun.

"Little Brother said turn her loose!" Quirt shouted from the top of the ramp.

"You again?" Shelby screamed.

"They got us surrounded," Painter moaned.

"They got nothin'. We ain't backin' down this time."

"Let her go!" Bronc shouted.

"Go to Hades," the tall one barked.

231

"You're surrounded, boys, throw down," Coosie declared.

"By cripples and a kid," Shelby sneered.

Painter pulled Miss Diane's arm behind her, and shoved the knife at her throat. "Back off!" he shouted.

"Get the box from the kid, Leon. And it better be crammed with hundred-dollar bills," Shelby hollered as he waved his gun at the cowboys.

"I ain't that stupid," Leon declared. "I put it in diamonds."

I stared into Miss Diane's blue eyes. "You're hurting my arm," she cried out.

Leon pointed at me. "The kid's got it. It's all dime-store jewelry except for . . ."

To this day I don't know what made me do it. I don't know if I was smart or dumb. Maybe it was the little-boy infatuation with the tall lady in the tight skirt. I like to think I was caught up with the cold courage I saw on the faces of six, old-time cowboys.

But maybe it was a nervous reaction by a ten-year-old too scared to pee.

I reached over the edge of the loading dock as if to hand the box to the charging Leon. Then I opened the lid on the White Owl box, and dumped the contents into the rain-soaked leaves and trash in the concrete ramp below.

Most of the contents landed a few feet from the storm drain.

"No!" Leon screamed and dove for the jewelry.

I tossed the box beside him and retreated behind the barrels.

"Don't let them go down the drain," he hollered. "Look for the diamond ring with the white-gold band. That's a ten-thousand-dollar ring."

Painter shoved Miss Diane to the wet concrete and scampered after the jewels.

Shelby froze.

On his knees, Leon scattered leaves and trash like a lawnmower running over the flowerbed. "Block off that storm drain."

Shelby shoved his gun in his Levi's and sprinted to the floating cigar box as it swirled towards the drain.

Quirt and Bronc, guns pointed at the robbers, trotted down the long ramp, Granddaddy right behind them.

They headed straight for Miss Diane.

"Get her out of here, Pop," Quirt hollered.

While he and Bronc shielded them, Granddaddy led a shaking Diane Anderson up the truck ramp to Shorty, Thad and Coosie.

CHAPTER 46

"Where is it?" the short one shouted on his hands and knees. "Is this it?"

Leon lunged through the dead, wet leaves. "I said diamond."

The shorter one dangled a bracelet from his fingers. "How do I know . . ."

"Stand up against that back wall, boys." Quirt flashed my badge. "You are under arrest."

"Oh, man," Leon groaned. "Why does this always happen to me?"

"I should have shot him this afternoon," Shelby barked. "There's three of us and only two of them down here. We can jump them."

"Jump them?" Painter whined. "They got guns. All of them has guns."

"Them washed-out old men couldn't hit a spittoon the size of a washtub from up there," Shelby snarled. He dropped the cigar box and grabbed for his handgun.

The blast came from the top of the ramp followed by a short puff of smoke from Coosie's gun.

All eyes were on the White Owl box, slammed against the back wall, a hole the size of a quarter blasted through the middle.

Leon and Painter jumped up, hands raised.

Shelby glared up the ramp, his right hand behind his back, resting on the grip of his pistol.

"Son, I'm the lousiest shot in the whole posse," Coosie shouted. "If you're thinkin' about usin' that gun, you'll have five bullets in your chest before your finger even squeezes the trigger."

It seemed like an hour of staring each other down. Finally, the robber dropped his gun in the leaves and held up his hands. "I don't believe this. Twice in the same day."

When the police siren blared, I rushed to where Grandpa stood. The black-and-white DeSoto slid to a stop. Two uniformed officers and Detective Tyler Young jumped out.

"It's about time you showed up," Miss Diane said.

"A pawn-shop hold-up. A couple of hoods stole guns and . . ."

"A knife with a pearl handle, I reckon." Thad nodded down at the three in the Pit.

The detective stared down the ramp. "You got them?"

"It wasn't much," Shorty said. "They ain't real smart."

The officers jogged down the ramp and hand-cuffed the three, then shoved them to the police car. Quirt and Bronc swaggered up behind them, guns now out of sight.

"Did they say anything about the stolen money?" the detective asked.

"They said it was converted to a diamond ring. That got dumped down there in the leaves and trash," Quirt explained. "Could be the Albuquerque storm drain is more valuable than most folks figure."

Detective Young pulled off his hat and rubbed his square forehead. "I'll get a city crew over here and we'll see what we can find."

"No need for that," I said.

"What do you mean, Little Brother?" Granddaddy asked.

I reached into the pocket of my damp jeans. "I was savin' this to give to Miss Diane. It was the only one in the box that cut the glass table." I chewed on my tongue and caught my breath. "I didn't aim to steal it. I just wanted to borrow somethin' to show Miss Diane 'cause she was feelin' low."

I handed the ring to the lady with the most beautiful blue eyes God ever created. She slipped it on the ring finger of her left hand.

"Little Brother, you are one amazing cowboy. I've never worn a ten-thousand-dollar ring." She held it out front for all the men to see. "Do you see what my little hero gave me? I was just born twenty years too soon." She pulled off the ring and handed it to the detective.

For the next half-hour, we huddled near the police car to provide details of the events. Miss Diane had me stand with her under the umbrella when it started to sprinkle again. Her right hand rested on the wet shoulder of my blue, gingham shirt.

There have been a few times in my life when I wished the moment lasted forever. This was one of the first of those times.

When we answered all the questions, Miss Diane accepted a ride to the police station to fill out further reports. The robbers and Leon were hauled off to jail. Me and the cowboys hiked across the alley to the back door of the Matador Hotel.

"That was fine shootin', Coosie," Bronc said.

Coosie patted his holstered revolver. "Boys, that's the last day I'm goin' to wear this gun. My shootin' days are over."

"What do you mean, over?" Thad said. "You stood a hundred feet away and fired off-hand and still hit that cigar box dead center. That's good shootin'."

"You weren't that good when you was young," Shorty added. "I remember down at that shootin' contest in Rio Verde you missed that watermelon six times and finally threw your pistol at it."

"They are exageratin', Little Brother. I only missed it five times. I never in my life carried six beans in the wheel," Coosie insisted.

"Then why are you goin' to put your gun away, Mr. Harte?" I asked.

" 'Cause I wasn't aimin' at the cigar box," Coosie stated. "I was aimin' at his gut."

CHAPTER 47

We moseyed back to the worn, brown leather chairs and sofa. Quirt disappeared into the back office. He emerged with a couple of towels, which soon got passed around. "There's a note back there that Emily is sick and went home early. I don't think anyone is runnin' the hotel."

Coosie stared around at the vacant lobby. "I reckon for a while there won't be much need for anyone."

Shorty dried off his thin, gray hair and tossed the towel to Grandpa. "Boys, I'll have to admit, that's more excitement than I've seen in quite a spell."

"I haven't had this much fun since that Brahmer bull jumped the fence at the Gallup Rodeo and plowed through Margarita's . . . eh . . ." Bronc glanced over at me. "Margarita's Dance Emporium."

"It's a shame they will lock up Leon. He can be quite entertaining," Granddaddy said.

"We can always drum up an exciting game of cribbage, boys," Coosie said.

Thad shrugged. "Just don't seem quite the same."

"You know, for a minute there, standin' around the Pit, I felt like a young man again," Quirt admitted.

Coosie laughed. "Shoot, you boys are young."

"I know what you mean," Bronc replied. "It was like we was doin' somethin' important."

"We were. We saved Miss Diane's life," I told them.

Coosie sighed, then pulled out his teeth. "I don't know if we did that, but it made me glad to be alive. It's rough, Little Brother, when you lose that feelin'."

Shorty stroked his long mustache. "Most days it's just like sittin' at the depot waitin' for a train that never arrives."

"I reckon Little Brother proved his salt today, boys." Quirt handed me back my tin deputy marshal's badge.

Bronc winked at me. "You'll do to ride the river with him."

"I dropped the box," I said.

"That was smart," Bronc said.

I took a deep breath and blew it out fast. "But, I was just scared and didn't know what else to do."

"Little Brother, that's exactly the way most acts of bravery occur. We get too scared to think things through, and instinct takes over," Bronc said.

"Bronc's right," Quirt Payton added. "That's when we got to rely on character, on courage, on reflexes that you trained durin' the easy times. It's the tough times, the dangerous times that show what you're made of. Most boys today don't have a clue what they are made of, 'cause they never been tested."

"Remember that bank teller in Durango?" Thad said.

Granddaddy nodded. "The skinny kid with thick glasses?"

"He looked the type the wind would blow over," Thad replied. "We had him pegged for a squeal-and-run man."

"We even joked about him over at the Castle Café. Said we'd never hire such a man to stand between the vault and our money," Coosie declared.

Quirt stared at the front door and shook his head. "Then Loudy LaFevere and that bunch busted in about closin' time and demanded the money. The kid refused. They shot him in both legs and still he refused."

"By then the marshal showed up and arrested them all. The kid pulled through. He ended up owning that bank," Granddaddy explained.

"You know why, Little Brother?" Bronc challenged.

My forehead wrinkled under my straw hat. I sensed I was suppose to know the answer. My mind went blank and I could only utter a weak, "Why?"

" 'Cause ever'one in the area trusted him to take care of their money from that moment on,"

Bronc said. "Yep, you don't know what a man's made out of until he'd been through the fire. You were tested today, Little Brother . . . and you passed."

Coosie grinned like a half-moon. "Not sure how you and Pop will explain this to Katie."

"I think I'll just let Little Brother tell his side of things. Katie will sigh and say, 'You shouldn't let those old men fill his head with yarns.' "

The bell over the front door jangled. A short man with dark-framed glasses pushed a suitcase into the hotel and used it as a door stop. "Excuse me, boy, can I get some help with these bags?" He disappeared back outside.

"Was he talking to me?" I gulped.

Quirt scratched his head. "I reckon we better run the hotel until Miss Diane gets back. Come on, Bronc, you and me can unload the bags. Pop, you and Coosie run the desk. Thad, you and Shorty are the inside bellhops."

"The Matador hasn't had bellhops in six years," Shorty complained.

"Yeah, but that ol' boy don't know it. Come on." Quirt headed for the door.

I trailed Grandpa and Coosie to the registration desk, while Shorty and Thad stood at attention near the stairway.

The short man with dark-framed glasses strolled in, hat in hand, followed by the widest woman I ever saw. And by then, I had seen the "Elephant

Lady of Borneo" at the Clyde Beatty Circus. She carried a tiny, black dachshund with a red velvet collar.

They marched to the desk.

"We would like the best room in the hotel," the man declared. "Money is no object."

Grandpa turned the ledger around. "Yes, sir, just fill in this information."

"The best room in the hotel is 308," Coosie declared. "It's a three-room suite with a small kitchen. It's ten dollars a night."

"Fine, I'll take that one."

"You'll have to check with Mrs. Williams."

"Is she the manager?" the man asked.

"No, she's the one in that room now. I ain't sure she wants company." Coosie rubbed his round chin. "But, it is the nicest room in the Matador."

The man curled eyebrows thicker than John L. Lewis'. "What is the nicest one that's available?"

"Room 321 has a nice view of the train yard. Three-thirty is a corner room. Both of them have their own bathrooms," Granddaddy said.

"I should hope so. We'll take the corner room," the man said.

Quirt and Bronc sat four, identical, brown Samsonite suitcases down behind the couple and waited.

"Tip the boys, Holbrooke," the lady insisted.

The man put a fifty-cent piece in each man's hand. "Take the bags to our room," he said.

"Sorry, we're the outside men." Quirt nodded toward Shorty and Thad at the stairway. "You'll have to use the bellboys."

"Boys?" the lady said.

Reaching for his wallet, the man in the dark suit and tie glanced over his shoulder. "We'll take our own bags up in the elevator."

"How many nights will you be staying?" Granddaddy asked.

"Until the dog show is over. Four nights," the lady reported.

Granddaddy pointed to a sign on the wall. "The normal procedure is to deposit one-half the fee in advance."

The man handed him a twenty-dollar bill.

"Does our room have a television set?" the lady asked. "Gretchen enjoys watching 'You Are There.' "

"Gretchen?" Coosie asked.

"Our dog," she replied.

"No, ma'am, the room doesn't have television," Granddaddy said. "There is no television in the hotel, but most rooms have a fine RCA radio."

"No television?" she whined. "Holbrooke, what will we do?"

"You can read Gretchen a story." He turned back to Granddaddy. "Is there anything else this hotel doesn't have?"

"It doesn't have an elevator," Coosie reported.

CHAPTER 48

Thad and Shorty returned to the lobby in a few minutes, both of them puffing, but grinning. They waved fifty-cent pieces, then tossed them to me.

"Little Brother gets the tips today," Shorty declared.

Bronc and Quirt handed me theirs, too. I glanced up at Granddaddy. He nodded his approval.

All seven cowboys stood when Miss Diane entered the lobby wearing a blue dress suit, white scarf and white gloves. "Detective Young was kind enough to take me by my place so I could change out of those wet clothes."

"He's a very helpful fellow," Quirt noted with a frown.

"And quite tall," she smiled as she tugged off the gloves. "My husband was a tall man."

"Havin' a lawman for a boyfriend can make you nervous, Miss Diane," Bronc remarked. "Jist ask Quirt."

"The right woman can settle a man down, I reckon," Quirt replied.

"Tyler said there will be nothing in the report about a shot fired at the Pit. That just complicates things. The short one and Leon confessed to everything, so he thinks they will stay in jail quite a while. Thanks to all of you and especially, Little Brother."

"Shucks, it was nothin', Miss Diane," I blurted out.

She laughed. "Did he just say 'Shucks, it was nothin' '?"

"I reckon we corrupted him some," Coosie said.

"I love it. He might be the youngest, old-time cowboy in captivity."

"We're tryin' to school him, Miss Diane," Shorty said. "He's a very fast learner."

"I can see that. I have something for you, Little Brother." She strolled over to me and my heart nearly stopped.

She held out a wide, brown envelope and pulled out a picture of her standing in front of the Matador Hotel.

"I had given it to Leon, but he didn't want it anymore. The detective let me take it. I think he was hoping I'd give it to him. But, I want you to have it, instead. Now turn it over."

"7-3099?"

"That's my phone number. I expect you to phone me in ten years and tell me how you are doing." She kissed her two fingers then pressed them against my cheek. "Thank you, Little Brother."

My cheek felt on fire and I thought it would melt right into my teeth. None of us sat down until Miss Diane strutted back to the office.

Thad Brewer broke into some story about a yellowed-haired lady named Pepper that he met when he was twelve . . . but I stared at the photo. To this day, I have every feature memorized. I taped that picture to my cherrywood desk at home. You know, the type that has a fold-down desktop and a bunch of pigeon holes? It hung with the picture of Roy Rogers, Gary Cooper and the Lone Ranger for a number of years. I never did phone Miss Diane although I thought about it a million times. I read in the paper that she married Detective Tyler Young about a year later. Shorty told me they moved to El Centro, California, and he was working for the Border Patrol.

The picture, along with the others, remained in the little drawer in that desk until my wife decided to refinish it. She asked me who the lady was and I said some movie star I met as a kid when I was visitin' my grandparents in Albuquerque. So she tossed it out.

I still have the pictures of Roy, Gary and the Lone Ranger.

But the image of Miss Diane is still in my mind and reminds me of a very good time in my life.

On that day, I slipped the picture in my shirt pocket, and re-pinned my tin deputy marshal's badge in front of it. The ruffle of cards yanked my thoughts back to the lobby of the Matador Hotel.

Coosie lounged in a leather chair, his round head tilted back, his toothless mouth open.

"I think Mr. Harte is asleep," I whispered.

Granddaddy pulled out his packet of cigarette papers and the little bag of tobacco. "I reckon he's dreamin' of ridin' the range, Little Brother. It's been a busy day. That's what happens when you get old."

"Coosie's always been a good sleeper," Shorty said. "Remember that time we all took the train from Casper, Wyoming, back to Lubbock?"

"I got kicked off in Pueblo," Bronc said. "Best thing that ever happened to me."

"You should have married that girl," Granddaddy commented.

"I know it, Pop. Hardly a day goes by when I don't say the same thing."

"Why did you get kicked off the train?" I asked.

Bronc scratched the back of his short-cropped, gray hair. "You want the long story or the short version?"

Granddaddy pulled his pocket watch out of his suit coat. "Give him the short version, Bronc. Katie don't cotton much to us bein' late for supper and she was promisin' sweet-potato pie."

Thad leaned back against the sofa, folded his big arms, and closed his eyes. "We're glad you got your Katie, Pop. It mollifies us some to know that at least one of us got it right."

CHAPTER 49

Bronc tugged on the button collar of his white shirt. "The days of the big cattle drives were long gone, Little Brother. But ever' once in a while there were still a few hundred head that needed to be delivered. So they kept a corridor of open range about one mile wide leadin' right up from Texas to Montana."

Thad Brewer leaned towards me. "There was bridges over the rivers."

"And an occasional automobile," Shorty McGuire added.

"It was surely one of the last drives north," Bronc continued. "But they had just opened up a big oilfield west of Casper. Boomtowns sprouted all over the prairie and them roustabouts wanted more beef than Wyoming could supply."

"They were raising too many sheep up there then," Quirt explained.

"A hard winter hit Wyoming and Montana," Bronc said, "so King Tavian hired us to . . ."

"You were hired by a king?" I interrupted.

"No, no. His first name was King," Bronc said. "Had a spread on the Texas–New Mexico border."

"He hired us to drive them north 'cause none of them kids had ever done it before," Shorty said. "Coosie ran the wagon. Quirt headed the crew."

"An Indian kid wrangled the horses. What was his name?" Thad pressed.

"Horatio Ham," Granddaddy stated.

Thad nodded. "That's him."

"He got killed in the Great War, did you know that?" Shorty said. "He was a good kid."

"I didn't know," Thad replied. "I'm sorry to hear it."

Bronc cleared his throat. "We drove them north. There was no Comanches, no Sioux, no rustlers, no packs of wolves. Shoot, we didn't even have a good storm."

Granddaddy patted my knee. "In other words, Little Brother, it was a very boring trip."

"We delivered the cattle to the stockyards west of Casper. King Tavian paid us off. He wanted to sell all the horses, so he bought us train tickets back to Texas. We had one night in Casper to clean up and buy some fresh duds, then we boarded the train," Bronc said.

Thad had a grin as wide as his girth. "One night in town ain't nearly enough to celebrate a cattle drive. So Bronc and me decided we'd finish our party on the train."

"We sat in the club car wettin' our tongues and playin' cards till mornin'," Shorty explained.

"You played cribbage all night long?" I asked.

Quirt tapped on the cribbage board. "That day I reckon we were playin' poker, Little Brother."

"About four in the mornin', we pulled into some little town in Wyoming or Colorado. They was diggin' trenches, so they had those little, tiny, black, smudge-pots burnin' to warn of the open trench, the type about the size of cantaloupe and looked like an old-fashion bomb." Bronc's deep voice grew louder. "Me and Quirt slid down a window and decided to see how many of them we could shoot as we roared past. As I recollect, I won."

"You remember wrong," Quirt said. "You were just under the weather by then and lost track counting mine."

"Anyway, the porters and conductor abandoned the club car to us. We was having a great time until we pulled into Greeley. Except for Coosie. He slept through the whole evenin'," Bronc said.

"In Greeley, the engineer came back and said he wouldn't move the train an inch unless we returned to our seats. We did, and most of us fell asleep for a few hours," Thad reported.

Shorty waved his hands like a fan. "It was July-hot and stuffy and we pushed them windows down."

"But it still wasn't very comfortable," Granddaddy expounded. "So someplace in southern Colorado, Bronc decided he'd sleep on top the Pullman car."

I stared at the cowboy with the unknown last name. "You slept outside on a movin' train?"

"When the train slowed around the corner, I crawled out the window and up on top," Bronc explained. "It was peaceful up there, Little Brother. I rolled up my jacket for a pillow and fell asleep."

Quirt took up the story. "Now all was goin' fine until we pulled into the outskirts of Pueblo. Someone reported seein' a train robber jump on top the mail car. A dozen deputies waited to arrest all of us."

"That's when Coosie woke up," Thad said. "He didn't have a clue what was going on, but heard someone shout 'train robbers.' So he pulled his gun to protect himself, just as the sheriff entered the car."

"It took a while," Granddaddy said, "to clear up the confusion. We had to store our guns in the satchel and leave them in the baggage car. Bronc showed them his ticket, but they said he violated railroad policy and booted him off."

Bronc leaned back, his arms folded. "I had some friends in Pueblo, so I didn't mind the layover."

"The rest of us rode the train back to Texas," Shorty stated. "But Coosie was afraid to go to sleep after that."

"My friends had a niece staying with them: Miss Adele Fernley. Me and her got close, but she had to go home to Indiana. She begged me to come back and meet her parents. I told her I had my fill of long train rides, and would just travel horseback to see her." Bronc paused and stared at the front door, his eyes a bit glazed.

I waited a respectful pause. "And you never did?"

Bronc leaned his elbows on his knees. "I bought me a fine horse and a pack horse. Rode east for two days. I camped outside some little Nebraska town one night and came to my senses. A lady like that needs a whole lot more than a washed-out cowboy. I was just kiddin' myself, I thought. Indiana would only be embarrassin' for me and for sweet Adele. So I turned south and caught up with Coosie and Shorty in El Paso."

"And you never saw her again?" I quizzed.

"I see her ever' night, Little Brother. She never grows old. Never has a blemish."

Thad shrugged. "Which is a whole lot more than we can say."

"I'd like to grow old," I said. "I mean, a little bit, anyway."

"You will soon enough, Little Brother. Some day you will look back and this rainy afternoon in Albuquerque will be a distant memory," Quirt mused.

Bronc hooted. "Shoot, he'll have so many adventures he won't even recall today."

"I'll remember," I insisted. "A man never forgets his friends."

Granddaddy stood and jammed on his hat. "Little Brother, say goodbye to your friends for now. Grandma will be sittin' on the screen porch watchin' the street, as it is. We don't want to keep her waitin'."

They either slapped my back or shook my hand. Coosie woke up long enough to give me that toothless, man-in-the-moon wink of his and promised to tell me about how Johnny Appleseed carved a gun out of lye soap.

Wearin' my straw hat, cap guns, and sportin' my new, tin badge, I swaggered to the front door of the Matador Hotel. Grandpa marched out to the street, but I turned around.

All five men tipped their hats to me.

I tipped mine back.

It turned out to be the only time I was ever with them all.

And that's the way it happened.

More or less.

When I was a cowboy for a rainy afternoon.

Center Point Publishing
600 Brooks Road ● PO Box 1
Thorndike ME 04986-0001 USA

(207) 568-3717

US & Canada:
1 800 929-9108
www.centerpointlargeprint.com